MARVEL
GUARDIANS OF THE GALAXY
Hallo-Scream Spook-Tacular!!!

Written by **Colin Hosten** and **Tomas Palacios**
Illustrated by **Michael Ryan** and **Chris Sotomayor**
Based on the Marvel comic book series
Guardians of the Galaxy

MARVEL
marvelkids.com

Printed in the United States of America
First Edition, July 2016
10 9 8 7 6 5 4 3 2 1
ISBN 978-1-4847-3214-4
FAC-029261-16148
Library of Congress Control Number: 2016932949

SUSTAINABLE FORESTRY INITIATIVE
Certified Sourcing
www.sfiprogram.org
SFI-01415

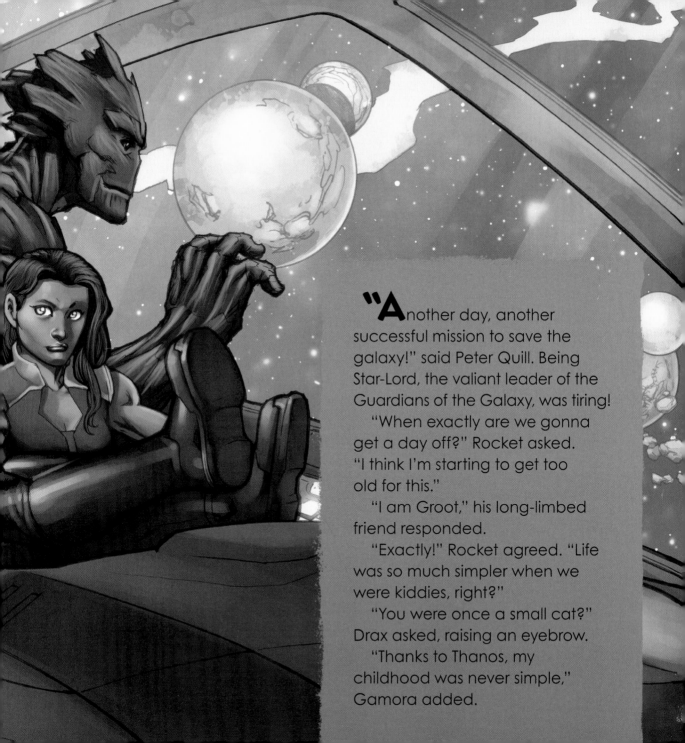

"**A**nother day, another successful mission to save the galaxy!" said Peter Quill. Being Star-Lord, the valiant leader of the Guardians of the Galaxy, was tiring!

"When exactly are we gonna get a day off?" Rocket asked. "I think I'm starting to get too old for this."

"I am Groot," his long-limbed friend responded.

"Exactly!" Rocket agreed. "Life was so much simpler when we were kiddies, right?"

"You were once a small cat?" Drax asked, raising an eyebrow.

"Thanks to Thanos, my childhood was never simple," Gamora added.

"I always loved Halloween," Peter said. "Dressing up like a pirate or a monster. I could be whatever I wanted! Not to mention all the candy I could eat!"

The other Guardians stared blankly at Peter.

"You have no idea what I'm talking about, do you?" he asked.

"Not a clue," Gamora replied.

"Snickers? Mars bars? Milky Way?"

"Mmmm," said Rocket, salivating. "It sounds like Candies of the Galaxy!"

"Yes! We even have ones that look like Infinity Stones. Ever heard of a Ring Pop?"

Groot raised his hand. "I am Groot."

"No, no, not like tree rings," Rocket said.

"Ring Pop!"

"I am Groot."

"Close enough," Peter sighed.

Drax grunted. "I like the sound of Candies of the Galaxy. When can we go?"

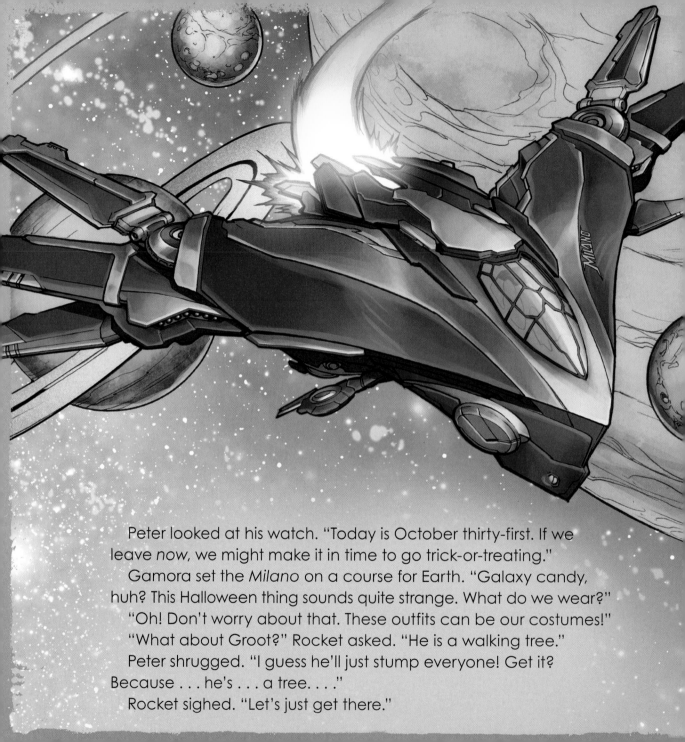

Peter looked at his watch. "Today is October thirty-first. If we leave *now*, we might make it in time to go trick-or-treating."

Gamora set the *Milano* on a course for Earth. "Galaxy candy, huh? This Halloween thing sounds quite strange. What do we wear?"

"Oh! Don't worry about that. These outfits can be our costumes!"

"What about Groot?" Rocket asked. "He is a walking tree."

Peter shrugged. "I guess he'll just stump everyone! Get it? Because . . . he's . . . a tree. . . ."

Rocket sighed. "Let's just get there."

The Guardians hid the *Milano* behind some trees and walked over to a sidewalk filled with trick-or-treaters. A space cowboy **zoomed** by with a laser gun, and a small ghost stuffed a lollipop in his mouth. A vampire cat walked by the Guardians and waved.

"Welcome to Springfield, New Jersey," said Peter.

The houses were covered with all kinds of decorations, including jack-o'-lanterns and fake skeletons, howling ghosts and green-faced witches.

"What happened to that one?" Rocket asked, pointing to a dark and scary-looking house at the end of the street.

"I dunno," Peter said with a smile. **"It must be . . . haunted."**

"Haunted?" said Rocket, crossing his arms. "You tryin' to scare me, Quill? We've fought aliens with purple hands and goofy teeth.

Nothin's gonna scare me!"

As Rocket finished, Drax snuck up behind him and playfully tickled him with a leaf. Rocket jumped as high as Groot's branches.

"Not funny, Drax!"

"Wow, you do have catlike reflexes!" Drax replied.

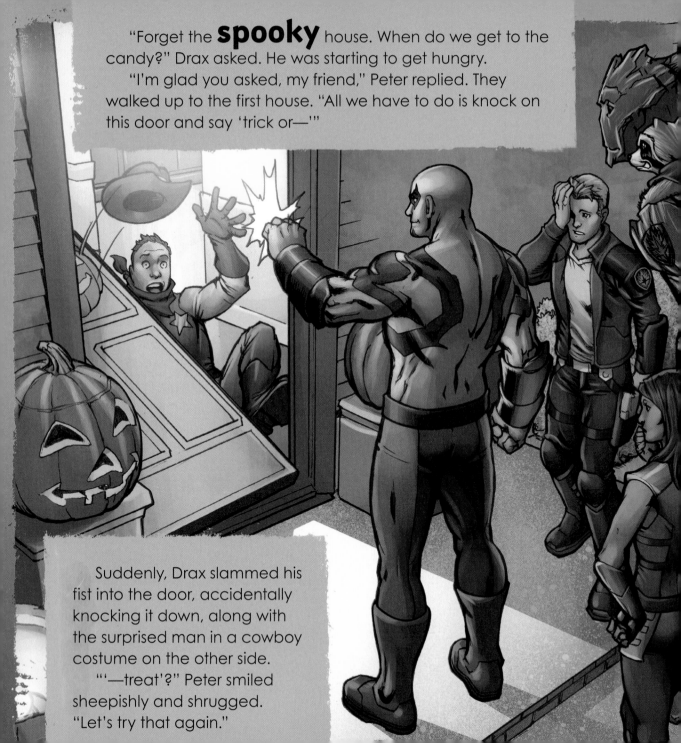

"Forget the **spooky** house. When do we get to the candy?" Drax asked. He was starting to get hungry.

"I'm glad you asked, my friend," Peter replied. They walked up to the first house. "All we have to do is knock on this door and say 'trick or—'"

Suddenly, Drax slammed his fist into the door, accidentally knocking it down, along with the surprised man in a cowboy costume on the other side.

"'—treat'?" Peter smiled sheepishly and shrugged. "Let's try that again."

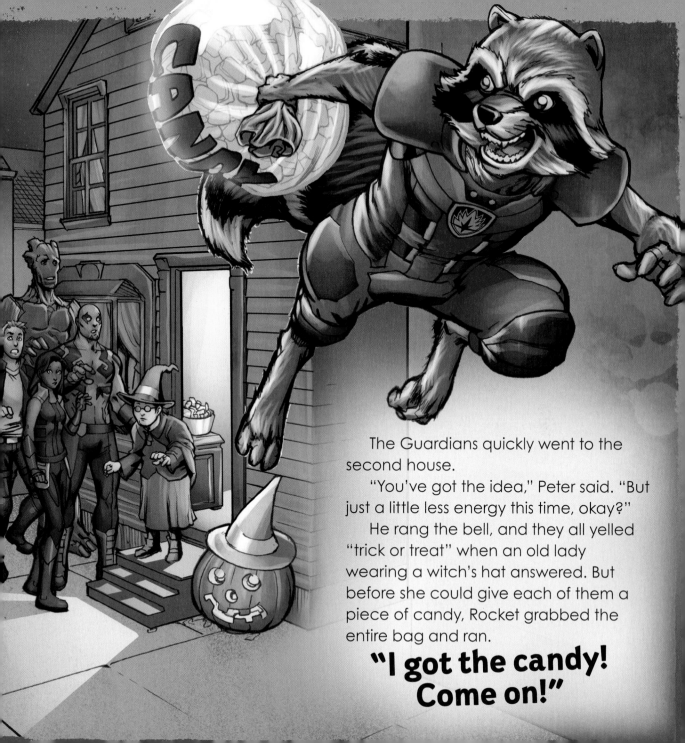

The Guardians quickly went to the second house.

"You've got the idea," Peter said. "But just a little less energy this time, okay?"

He rang the bell, and they all yelled "trick or treat" when an old lady wearing a witch's hat answered. But before she could give each of them a piece of candy, Rocket grabbed the entire bag and ran.

"I got the candy! Come on!"

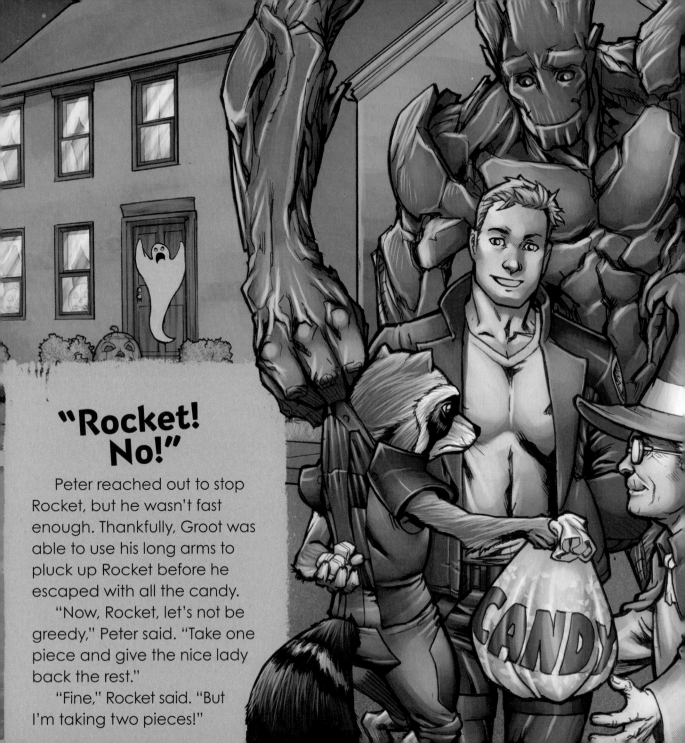

"Rocket! No!"

Peter reached out to stop Rocket, but he wasn't fast enough. Thankfully, Groot was able to use his long arms to pluck up Rocket before he escaped with all the candy.

"Now, Rocket, let's not be greedy," Peter said. "Take one piece and give the nice lady back the rest."

"Fine," Rocket said. "But I'm taking two pieces!"

"This is actually not so bad, Peter," Gamora said, unwrapping her candy bar as they walked to the next house. "I think I might like this Halloween thing."

Again, they rang the bell. This time, a man who looked like a skeleton opened the door.

"Watch out, he's dangerous!" Gamora yelled, grabbing the man by his shirt and lifting him up.

The other Guardians had to hold her back before she tossed him to the ground.

"Sorry about that, sir," Peter said. "Nice, uh, *costume*."

As they made their way to the next house, a group of costumed children walked up beside them.

"Wow, your parents are really cool," a boy in a shark costume whispered to Rocket. "My parents never get so dressed up for Halloween."

"'Scuse me?" Rocket said with attitude. "Exactly how old do you kids think I am?"

They looked at each other and shrugged. "Eight? Nine?"

A girl dressed as a dinosaur ballerina pulled on Rocket's whiskers. "You almost look like a real raccoon!"

Rocket jerked his head back.

"Hey! I ain't no raccoon, kid!"

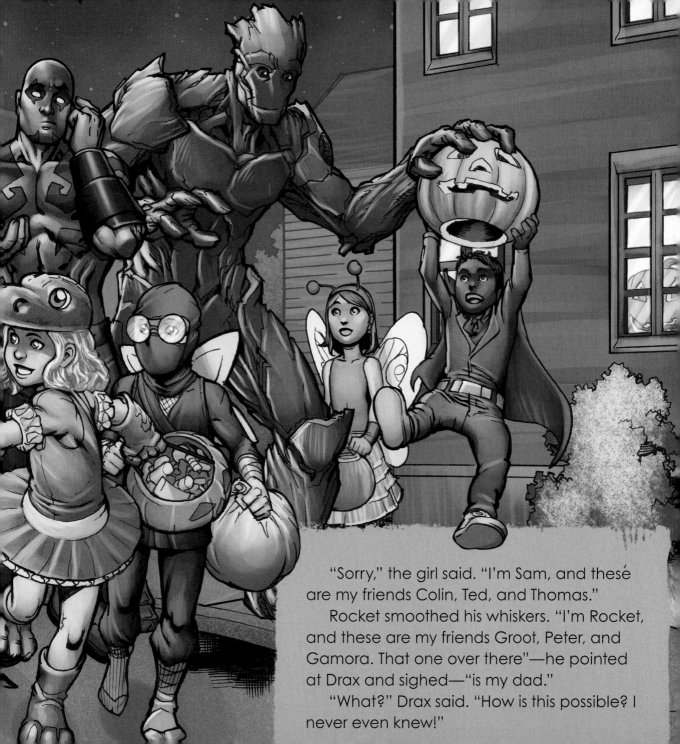

"Sorry," the girl said. "I'm Sam, and thesé are my friends Colin, Ted, and Thomas."

Rocket smoothed his whiskers. "I'm Rocket, and these are my friends Groot, Peter, and Gamora. That one over there"—he pointed at Drax and sighed—"is my dad."

"What?" Drax said. "How is this possible? I never even knew!"

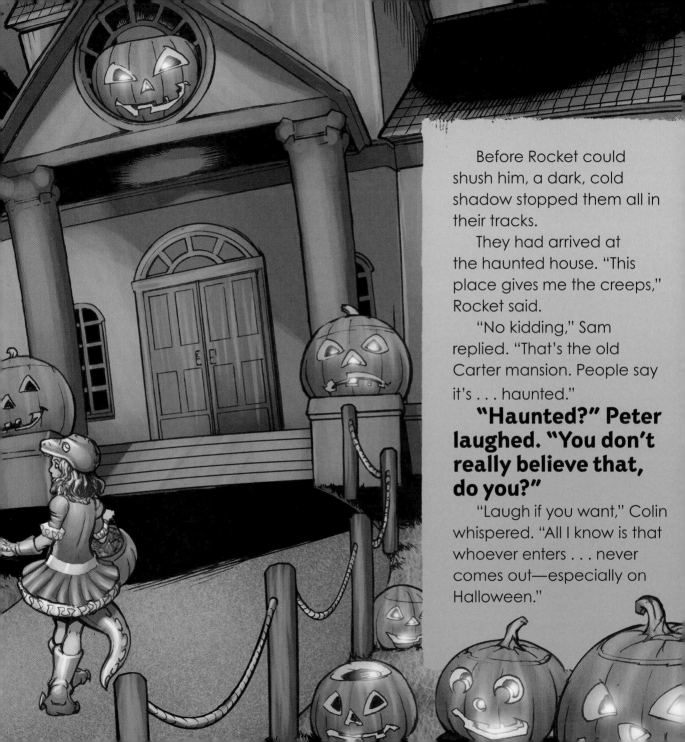

Before Rocket could shush him, a dark, cold shadow stopped them all in their tracks.

They had arrived at the haunted house. "This place gives me the creeps," Rocket said.

"No kidding," Sam replied. "That's the old Carter mansion. People say it's . . . haunted."

"Haunted?" Peter laughed. "You don't really believe that, do you?"

"Laugh if you want," Colin whispered. "All I know is that whoever enters . . . never comes out—especially on Halloween."

Sam looked around and realized someone was missing! "Oh, no! Where's Ted?"

"I think he's in there . . ." Thomas said in horror.

"If Ted is in there, we have to go in and find him!" Peter closed his fingers around his holstered Element Gun. "Besides, I want to see what all the fuss is about. Who's with me?"

"I am Groot!"

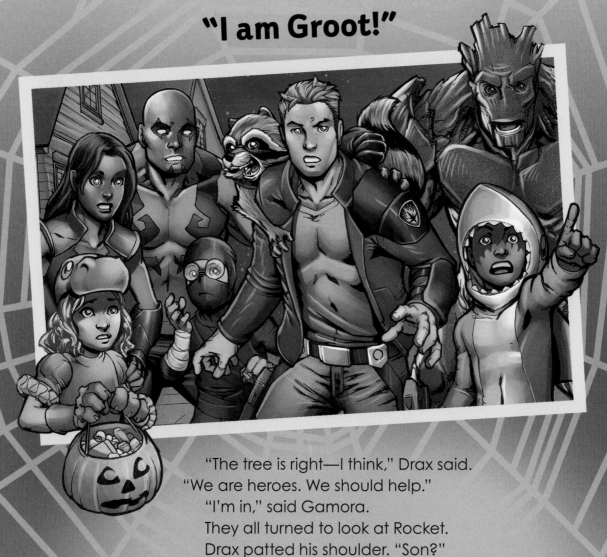

"The tree is right—I think," Drax said. "We are heroes. We should help."

"I'm in," said Gamora.

They all turned to look at Rocket.

Drax patted his shoulder. "Son?"

"All right, all right! Let's go in already!"

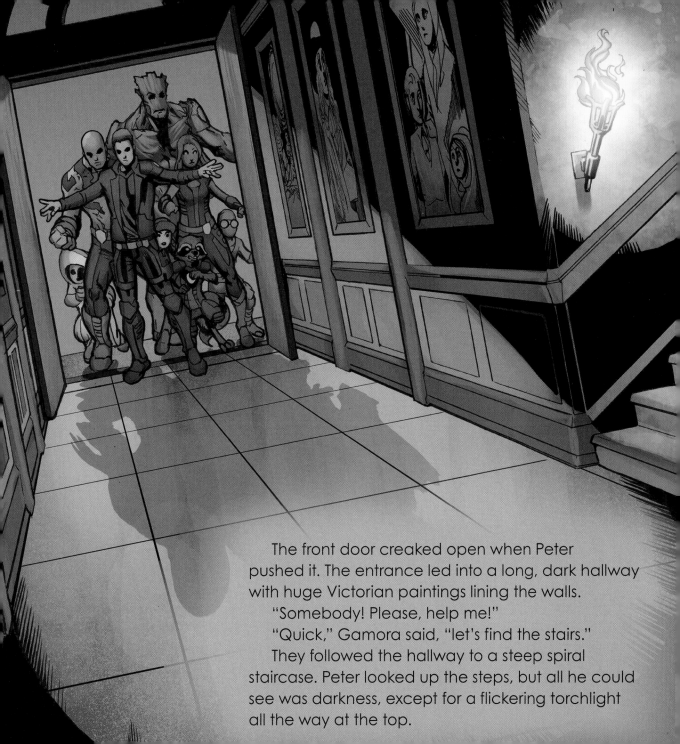

The front door creaked open when Peter
pushed it. The entrance led into a long, dark hallway
with huge Victorian paintings lining the walls.
    "Somebody! Please, help me!"
    "Quick," Gamora said, "let's find the stairs."
    They followed the hallway to a steep spiral
staircase. Peter looked up the steps, but all he could
see was darkness, except for a flickering torchlight
all the way at the top.

Upstairs, Drax took the torch off the wall and held it up to light the entire room. Peter gasped.

"Holy moly..."

There were a number of glass cases lining each wall, but the items on display weren't scientific artifacts. They were human beings! Most were children, and all of them were wearing unique costumes.

"There's Ted!" Thomas said, pointing to a hot dog in one of the glass cases.

Groot tapped on the glass, but the children seemed to be in some sort of suspended animation.

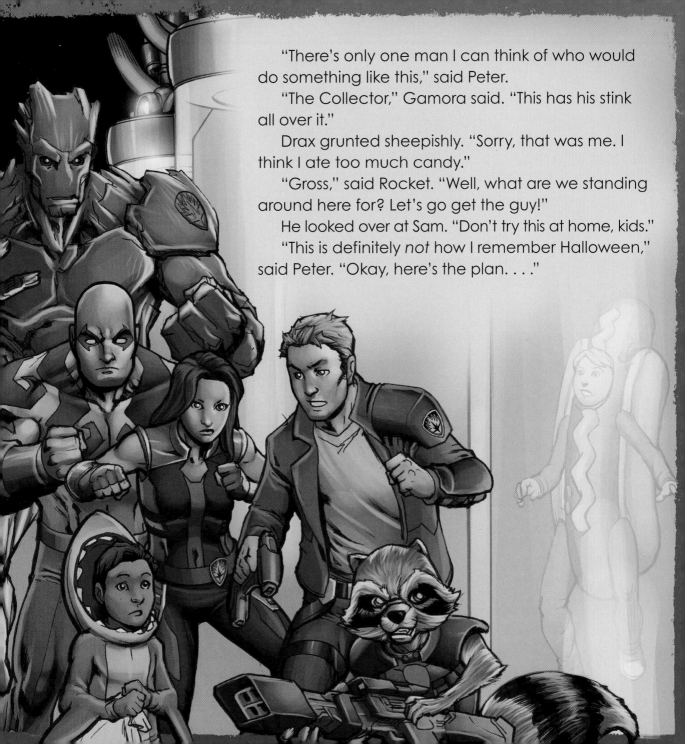

"There's only one man I can think of who would do something like this," said Peter.

"The Collector," Gamora said. "This has his stink all over it."

Drax grunted sheepishly. "Sorry, that was me. I think I ate too much candy."

"Gross," said Rocket. "Well, what are we standing around here for? Let's go get the guy!"

He looked over at Sam. "Don't try this at home, kids."

"This is definitely *not* how I remember Halloween," said Peter. "Okay, here's the plan. . . ."

A few moments later, the door opened and the Collector entered. The Guardians had already escaped.

"Well, well, what do we have here? Are you lost, little ones?"

"We're just looking for our friend, mister," said Sam. "We think he came in here."

"I'm sure I can help you find him," said the Collector. "I think I saw him just through these doors."

As he turned to lead the children away, one of the figures on display jumped to life. It was Rocket!

"Trick or treat!"

The Collector tried to grab Sam, but then Drax jumped out of another case, followed by Gamora and Groot.

"Give it up. You're surrounded." Star-Lord emerged from a case with his Element Gun aimed at the Collector. "Whatever madness you're planning here is over."

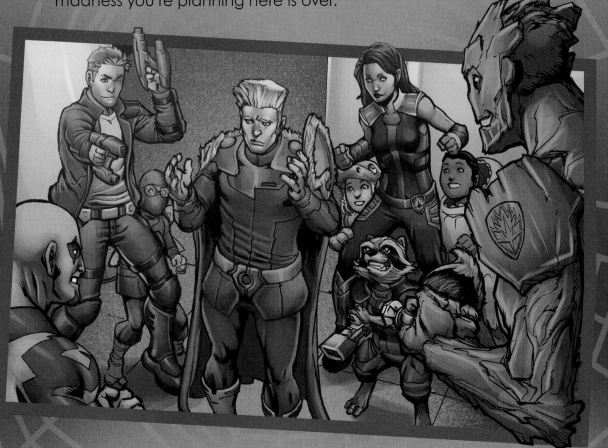

"'Madness'?" the Collector growled. "I'm making a museum! A museum of Earth's costume masterpieces!"

Gamora tied him up while the rest of the Guardians freed the children. "Halloween's not about museums!" she shouted. **"It's about candy!"**

"I am Groot!"

"Right, Groot," Rocket said. **"And Ring Pops!"**

Peter looked at his watch. "Halloween's not over yet—and I know exactly how we should celebrate!"

The Guardians and their new friends made the short trip to New York for the annual Halloween parade. Their costumes were the biggest hit with the crowd.

"Wow—that's the most lifelike raccoon I've ever seen!" someone said.

"How many times do I have to say it? I ain't no raccoon!"

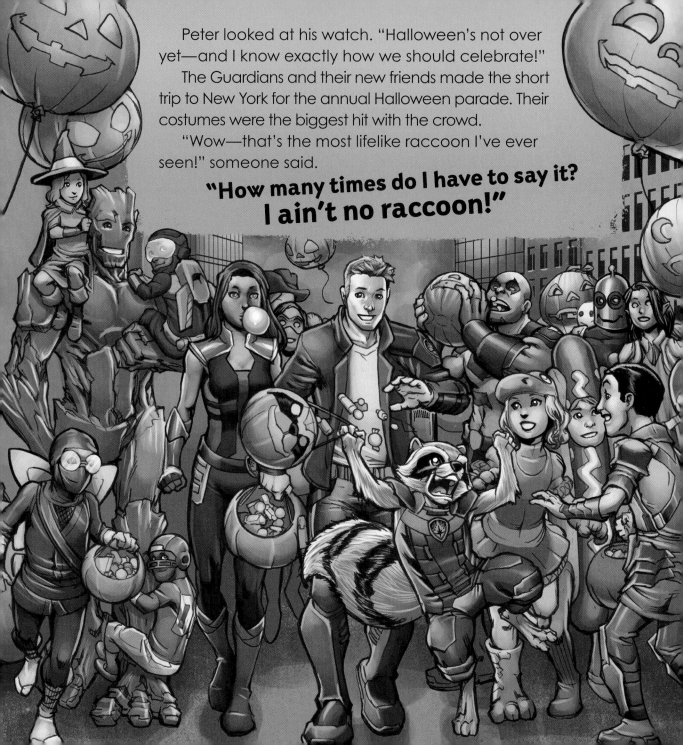

appears, then, that internal drives may be largely responsible for the
f superpower relations. For example, the domestic legitimacy of the
regime may be partly contingent on its ability to inspire fear and respect
, particularly since the regime's performance in domestic areas, such as
onomy, has not been especially impressive. Bureaucratic politics and
zational momentum also influence the course of Soviet behavior. In the
States, the power of the national-security bureaucracies probably
hes a limit beyond which improvements in superpower relations cannot
east in the short run. In this respect, it is probably fair to say that the na-
ecurity establishments of the two superpowers are each other's implicit
Nikita Khrushchev once told Norman Cousins, the author and publisher:
generals need each other. [The arms race] is the best way they have of
hening their positions and making themselves important." When Cous-
ayed this observation to President John F. Kennedy, the latter agreed.[1]
uch of the hostility between the two countries is rooted in fundamental
larities—cultural, political, and economic. However, these dissimilarities
not give rise to animosity were it not that both nations believe that their
alues have universal applicability, so that the rival's very existence and
represent a challenge to each side's pretensions. The psychological
nism that seeks to establish cognitive consistency then reinforces mutual
and distrust: If the other side stands for so much that is contrary to our
alues, it is satisfying to believe that its international behavior is contrary
interests. Consequently, we respond to the other side in a hostile manner,
onfirming the other side's worst suspicions and creating a self-perpetuat-
cle of hostility and distrust.

the tension in U.S.-Soviet relations arose from objectively competing
ts, it could be relieved by a compromise of some sort or by one side's
onment of that which is incompatible with the other's interest. But if it is
ed that much of the tension grows out of drives internal to the two
es, reinforced by their dissimilarities and by the psychological conse-
es of those dissimilarities, then a solution is much harder to envisage and
probably be extremely difficult to implement. None of this implies that
s no way out of the morass of superpower rivalry, but it does suggest that
antial amount of political will and great reserves of patience would be
ed. While working to improve superpower relations over the long term, a
r of immediate challenges must be met. The most pressing tasks are to
se the likelihood of nuclear conflict, to achieve meaningful arms control,
restrict the use of military force in the pursuit of Cold War advantages
developing world.

hreat of Nuclear War

ost people are not thrown into a permanent state of anxiety by the
of nuclear war. Partly, this is because we have become inured to the
by having been exposed to it for so long (many of us for our entire life-

phase, covering the decades preceding full-scale military involvement in
Vietnam, Congress was loath to involve itself in external affairs or to challenge
the decisions made by the president and his administration. It was virtually
obsequious toward the executive branch and abstained from playing a
meaningful foreign policy role. Its passive and uncritical acquiescence to the
interventions in Korea and, at first, in Vietnam clearly illustrated its attitude.

Beginning in the late 1960s, the legislators shook off their reticence, and a
new congressional disposition emerged. The conflict in Vietnam played a
catalytic role. As it escalated and as its high costs became more apparent,
members of Congress became increasingly aware of the dangers of allowing the
executive branch a free hand in foreign affairs, especially where possible
military involvements were concerned. The fact that both the Johnson and the
Nixon administrations had deceived the nation about the circumstances of the
U.S. military presence in Southeast Asia, and the public outrage that ensued,
emboldened Congress to assume a more activist role in foreign affairs. The
strongest indication of the changed outlook was the passage, in 1973, of the
War Powers Act, which significantly restricted the president's ability to
commit U.S. troops to foreign conflicts. Congressional oversight of covert
activities abroad was also strengthened. With the Arms Export Control Act of
1976, Congress also established a measure of legislative control over arms
transfers abroad. The Case Act of 1972 limited the executive branch's ability to
bypass, via executive agreements, congressional control over international
treaties. Dismayed by the repressive political practices of some of the nation's
Third World allies, Congress restricted the flow of economic and military
assistance to governments that systematically violated basic human rights. It
also demonstrated an increasing willingness to reject presidential foreign policy
appointees of whom it disapproved.

Subsequently, some people began to feel that the pendulum had swung
too far in the opposite direction and that the president's ability to conduct a
flexible and effective foreign policy was being unreasonably hampered by
congressional restrictions. The dangers of legislative meddling, they feared, had
come to outweigh the perils of unconstrained presidential power. Nevertheless,
Congress seems unwilling to return to the role of a passive spectator where
foreign affairs are concerned. If the executive branch departs from guidelines
that Congress deems appropriate, Congress will exercise its constitutional
prerogatives. However, legislators have many political concerns that are
unrelated to foreign policy, and their resources for monitoring the minutiae of
external affairs are limited. Thus, Congress does not feel impelled to exercise
the full range of its powers on a continuous basis or to involve itself in the daily
details of international relations. It has limited its role to preventing egregious
departures from basic goals and accepted methods. This seems like a reasonable
position and one that is compatible both with the principles of democratic
control and with the need for effective executive management of foreign
policy.

Thus far, the conduct of foreign policy in the United States does not seem to be drastically out of line with basic principles of democratic policy making. Contrary to what is sometimes thought, the public is not irrelevant to the process, and Congress does participate in what is probably the most appropriate way. Thus, the first of the three democratic principles (direct or indirect public participation) appears to be in reasonable harmony with the making of external policy. Nor does congressional involvement in international affairs represent much of a hindrance to flexible and dynamic external policy. In any case, a lesser congressional role would probably place more power in the hands of the executive branch than would be compatible with democratic principles and would provide real potential for abuses of the sort witnessed during the Vietnam War. One such abuse may be a disregard for certain basic liberties. The Nixon administration's program of spying on U.S. citizens who opposed the Vietnam War effort, President Lyndon B. Johnson's lies regarding the nature and circumstances of the nation's military involvement, and the "misinformation" campaigns directed toward the press during the Reagan administration (even if meant theoretically to confuse the country's adversaries) show that vigilance is still needed to ensure that democratic practices are followed in the execution of foreign policy.

The Bureaucracy and Private Power

The reassertion of congressional control over the executive branch in matters of foreign policy is relevant also to the second principle of democratic policy making—that there should be limits to the power of any one branch of government and of any single private group—but there is more to the problem than that. In particular, questions have been raised about the influence of the governmental bureaucracies and of powerful organized private interests that are not effectively countered by other private organizations or by public authority.

Much of what emerges as national policy is the product of the routines, preferences, and intramural wranglings of the foreign policy bureaucracy. These often invisible forces tend to escape legislative control and, to a large extent, presidential control as well. The precise effects of this phenomenon, which is inherent in the nature of large organizations, are not well understood. The bureaucracy's major influence lies not in its ability to undertake significant policy initiatives, but in its tendency to promote policies that enhance its own missions and resources, with little or no regard for their bearing on the interests of the nation as a whole. In addition, there is the danger that bureaucratic agencies whose work requires a degree of secrecy will operate entirely outside the purview of meaningful political control. Fears that this would be (or had been) the case with the CIA led to the initiation of congressional oversight of covert activities. More recently, it has come to light that the staff of the National Security Council negotiated with Iran on trading arms for hostages, in clear contravention of official policy, and that proceeds from arms sales to Iran

were used to fund activities of the Nicaraguan contras existing legislation—yet President Reagan was said unaware that this was being done. There are not man the violence they do to democratic practices is obvic

As for private interests, certain segments of the bu organized labor, as well as a number of ethnic lobbies, a substantial impact on foreign policy. Acting occasiona of the executive or legislative branches, they seek to sh consonant with their own interests rather than with whole. It would not be accurate to say that private l policy, but their relative power sometimes exceeds the cietal interests they represent.

The conclusion thus far is that, while there incompatibility between the requisites of democracy a effective foreign policy, the two occasionally have an problems have not reached such proportions that either policy is threatened, but the possibility cannot be i neither the dilemma of aggregation nor the dilemma c been fully resolved.

Security, Peace, and Military

East-West Hostility

An understanding of the sources of hostility and coi foundation for effective policies of peace and security. Soviet relationship, the explanations that serve as the bas surprisingly superficial. We saw that enmity between from two kinds of causes: a primary complex of circum rivalry and the secondary conditions that reinforce it. A the initiating causes may fade away and the animosity r the secondary causes alone.

In the case of the United States and the Soviet Unio identify objective conflicts of interest that might be the hostility. Neither territorial nor economic competition Ideological contention is clearly not irrelevant, but its ef exaggerated. The Soviet Union would almost certainly pr after its own image, but it seems unwilling to undertake such a world. Moreover, the pursuit of radical po developing nations seems less important to the Kr pragmatic foreign policy goals. Indeed, both superpowe considerable capacity to get along with nations that antithetical to their own when it appears to be to their advantage to do so.

time). Also, the sheer magnitude of the destruction that it would cause is such that there is nothing in our experience to which it can be compared, and it is hard to grasp the significance of something for which we have no experiential reference. Nevertheless, it is impossible to appreciate one of the most critical challenges facing U.S. foreign policy without understanding the nature of the nuclear peril.

Nuclear war is probably not survivable in any meaningful sense, nor can a nuclear war be fought on a limited scale in the pursuit of finite political and military goals, for we do not know how to fine-tune the use of nuclear weapons, and even their initially limited use is likely to engender an uncontrollable process of escalation. These facts are not always acknowledged in contemporary strategic doctrine, but an assessment of the effects of nuclear detonations—in terms of human losses, environmental damage, and economic and sociopolitical impact—can lead only to the conclusion that nuclear war would not be manageable or acceptable.

There are three paths which might lead to nuclear war: an accident, a preemptive first strike, and the escalation of a conventional conflict. An accident could be either the inadvertent launching of a weapon because of a physical malfunction or an unauthorized action by an individual military commander. But both these contingencies seem remote. Nuclear conflict is least likely to begin as the result of an accident.

In a situation of crisis instability, one side or the other could be tempted to launch a crippling preemptive first strike against its adversary. This temptation may have increased because of the dual effect of MIRV deployment and increased warhead accuracy. Because of this, the survivability of submarine forces is especially important, since they may represent the final strategic deterrent to a preemptive attack. However, major investments are currently being made in the technology of antisubmarine warfare, and if submarines should become vulnerable, the danger of nuclear war through a first strike during a crisis will become greater.

Perhaps the most likely road to nuclear war leads through a conventional conflict, possibly in Central Europe or the Middle East. History provides many examples of conflicts that escalated far beyond what the adversaries had intended, and there are strong psychological and military imperatives that encourage escalation. (The acceptance of the limited use of nuclear weapons in strategic doctrine could considerably narrow the gulf between conventional conflict and all-out nuclear devastation.) The threat of war via escalation imposes a heavy burden on superpower diplomacy: It must avoid petty provocations and gratuitous insults, muster the political will to establish constructive relations with the other side, and resist the tendency to confuse mutually negotiated security with an implicit endorsement of the other side's political system. In addition, there are specific steps that can be taken to reduce the risk of nuclear conflict, such as establishing an effective crisis control center, creating nuclear weapon-free zones, and maintaining submarine survivability.

The Arms Race

Many of the threats with which the two superpowers must deal are the product of the strategic arms competition, which has brought about the MIRVing of nuclear missiles, increases in the accuracy with which they can be delivered, and the creation of arsenals of nuclear weapons deemed appropriate for "limited" military applications. These technological developments have increased the number of conditions in which nuclear weapons could be used. Thus, the challenge of eliminating the possibility of nuclear warfare cannot be separated from that of controlling the arms race, and once again, arms control cannot be achieved unless the causes behind the military rivalry are understood.

The arms race has been blamed on the inherent drive of societies to arm, the machinations of a military-industry complex, or the inherent ill will and aggressiveness of the Soviet Union (or, from the Soviet viewpoint, of the United States). Actually, it is propelled by a complex combination of causes. The hypothesis of an inexorable cycle of response and counter-response, from which neither side can escape without at least short-term security losses, has been shown to be only partially valid. Each side does feel that it must respond to the significant military moves of its adversary, but each will in addition undertake new programs and activities even in the absence of initiatives by the other side. Thus, the causes of the arms race are not only external but also, like the superpower rivalry itself, internal—that is, connected to domestic forces within the two nations.

One of these forces is the structure of political rewards within both the United States and the Soviet Union. Their leaders are more severely punished in their own political system for understating the danger from the adversary than for overstating it. In the former case, they can be charged with irresponsibly imperiling the nation's security; in the latter case, at most, with expending too many resources on military preparedness. Faced with disproportionate punishments for the two sorts of errors, the rational politician will be more inclined to encourage than to discourage military growth and, as this is firmly embedded in the political system, it cannot be easily changed.

Another domestic force behind U.S.-Soviet hostility is the pressure of bureaucracies whose interests are tied to the military rivalry. Military bureaucracies derive their organizational power and resources from growing defense budgets and programs, and these bureaucracies are more powerful than those whose organizational interests are served by downplaying the military dimension of East-West relations. These are realities of the U.S. polity and, to an even greater degree, of the Soviet Union's; accordingly, bureaucratic interests will continue to represent an obstacle to arms control in the future.

In the United States, patterns of military growth are also linked to economic rhythms. Moreover, the interests of military producers are to some degree allied to those of the military bureaucracies. Technology also serves as an independent and powerful drive behind the military rivalry. Consequently, as new military possibilities are revealed in research laboratories and on testing ranges, a coalition of interests forms to ensure that the new development will lead to a deployed military system. As is the case with the threat of first strikes, technological innovations influence the strategic alternatives available to the superpowers, and they also shape the strategic doctrines that provide justification for the acquisition of new weapons and the guidelines for their use. The emergence of counterforce nuclear strategy as the accepted doctrine has largely been the result of such developments as the increasing number and accuracy of nuclear weapons and their decreasing size.

The forces behind the military rivalry are numerous, complex, and powerful, but this does not mean that they cannot be controlled or weakened. There are several ways in which this could be achieved, and budgetary constraints clearly place a ceiling on military spending within both societies. Still, U.S.-Soviet hostility must be mitigated where possible and circumvented where it cannot be reduced or eliminated. Ways of checking the domestic drives behind the arms race must be found, and the principle of congressional and presidential supremacy over the national bureaucracy must be affirmed. Negotiated restraints on weapons testing may help control the technological push toward military growth.

At the very beginning of this book, it was pointed out that military power could serve three functions: defense, deterrence, and compellence. The risks of uncontrollable escalation make nuclear weapons unsuited for the limited political purpose of compellence, even if they are appropriate for deterring a Soviet nuclear attack upon the United States, and perhaps on Western Europe. However, compellence with conventional military means may, under certain conditions, be an instrument of U.S. foreign policy, and it is important to consider what these conditions might be.

Nonnuclear Coercion

For a nation which has not itself been subject to hostile attacks, the United States has been involved in quite a few military conflicts. The two largest were, of course, World War I and World War II, but the nation has also used its military forces on a more limited scale several times since the end of World War II. These interventions have been associated with the pursuit of a Cold War goal somewhere in the developing world. In Korea, Vietnam, Lebanon, the Dominican Republic, and Grenada, the apparent aim was to counter a Soviet attempt at acquiring a geopolitical advantage at the expense of the United States. In Korea and Vietnam, interventions that were supposed to produce relatively quick and cheap victories, as well as political solutions favorable to U.S. interests, lasted far longer and claimed many more lives than anticipated. In Korea, the ultimate outcome was inconclusive; in Vietnam, it was an unambiguous defeat. Neither of the two military involvements in Lebanon produced a clearly favorable outcome. In the Dominican Republic and

Grenada, the United States achieved its objectives at moderate cost. There are lessons to be learned from these instances of armed intervention.

The first conclusion is that armed force has been effective only in cases where the balance of military power was so disproportionately tilted toward the United States that there could be no doubt whatsoever about the outcome. Success has also come when the political stakes were simple and straightforward and loyalties were clearly and easily defined. But such situations are exceptional and, in the majority of cases, the outcome is less likely to be favorable. It may be, as in Lebanon, that the political situation is too murky and fluid for there to be any lasting military solution beneficial to U.S. interests. In other cases, as in Korea and especially Vietnam, the costs may be much greater than expected with no favorable political solution within reach. Nevertheless, there are three mechanisms that can draw the country more deeply into a military involvement than any objective definition of the stakes would have justified. These are the logic of sunken costs, the logic of committed credibility, and the logic of domestic politics; their effect must be guarded against.

Few people believe that the nation should never resort to conventional military force. Armed force has a major role to play in deterring an enemy attack on the United States and its allies and in defending them should deterrence fail. It is also necessary to the protection of such U.S. interests as freedom of the seas and continued access to essential raw materials. More often, however, the situation is less clear-cut. It often involves a left-wing force, somewhere in the Third World, which shows a disregard for private property and political pluralism. This force may be the government in power, or it may threaten the continued incumbency of a government that is palatable to the United States. It may be overtly linked to the Soviet Union, or the possibility of such a link may be feared. In addition, the country in question may be located in a region to which some geopolitical importance is attached. The demands of containment and military credibility might then make armed intervention seem necessary in order to eliminate the perceived threat.

Still, recent U.S. experience shows that political reality is often too complex, slippery, and obstinate to be altered by guns and rockets. Coercion can lead to the physical removal of individuals and sometimes to the (perhaps temporary) destruction of institutions. But it cannot, as a rule, change political values or modify deeply rooted social aspirations and movements. Moreover, the political effects of military intervention can be unpredictable. It was almost certainly not anticipated that the intervention in Korea would lead to the involvement of Chinese forces. Even worse, it can be plausibly argued that the U.S. presence in South Vietnam actually did much to *strengthen* the hand of the Viet Cong, which, in the eyes of many Vietnamese, came to be identified with the struggle against an alien presence. Military intervention thus often changes the very nature of the situation, and political objectives become fluid and moving targets, compounding the dilemma of effective choice. The difficulties may be exacerbated by the fact that the local conditions that the military force is supposed to alter are not clearly understood. Political leaders often prefer simple explanations of foreign reality, with identifiable good and bad sides and simple and stable solutions. Moreover, there is no reason to suppose that any nation's political decision makers possess the cultural insights, political sensitivity, and wealth of factual knowledge required to fully understand conditions in distant societies. In any event, the contexts in which military force is supposed to achieve its objectives may not have sufficiently close historical parallels to provide useful guidelines for action. Thus, even where narrow military objectives are achievable at acceptable cost, political goals may remain disappointingly evanescent.

The conclusion is that military intervention is usually far more costly than anticipated and often unable to achieve political goals abroad. Even in those cases where the United States has managed to achieve its goals via armed force, an additional question must be raised: Is the objective worth the legitimation of military coercion as an instrument of foreign policy? When the United States resorts to coercion, it deprives itself of the moral authority to condemn the use of coercion by others. It might complain on other grounds (for example, the damage done to international stability), but not on the ground that military coercion is an unacceptable instrument of foreign policy.

Regional political goals need not, however, be abandoned, for there are other, more appropriate, ways of pursuing them. Diplomacy is one, though it requires patience and is most useful when the gap between interests is not overly great. Bribery through economic assistance will occasionally prove effective, though it, too, has its limitations—there are many examples of nations that have benefited from U.S. largess but have not reciprocated with political support. In some cases, the realization that military coercion is too costly and risky while diplomacy and bribery may not be effective leads decision makers to rely on methods located in a "middle ground" between the two: principally economic coercion and subversion through the informal penetration of other societies. Here, the record is mixed.

One difficulty with economic sanctions is that, because of the extent of economic interdependence between nations, it is not always possible to hurt an adversary without also hurting oneself as well as other nations. Thus, it is hard to use economic sanctions to produce narrowly targeted effects. Moreover, they do not always yield the desired results. The goal may be to weaken a foreign government by imposing economic pain on the country (as in the case of U.S. sanctions against Cuba and Nicaragua), but the result may be that the national hardships thus created provide the government with an excuse to tighten the reins of domestic control, or, in the face of foreign pressure, the public might actually rally around a government it would otherwise have opposed. Economic sanctions do occasionally work, but more often than not the results fall short of expectations.

The use of subversion has troublesome implications from the point of view of U.S. political practice, for it is, by its very nature, of doubtful compatibility with the principles of democratic policy making. It is, however, less costly, in both lives and money, than military intervention. Thus, it may be applicable to cases in which the stakes do not merit military involvement but are substantial enough to justify some strong action. Also, subversion has at times produced the desired results, as for example in Chile in 1973, when it brought about the removal of a leftist government (though it did not bring democracy to the country). On the other hand, subversion has its record of failures as well, ranging from attempts to get rid of Castro to efforts at influencing the elections in a number of democratic states. At times, these attempts have backfired dramatically, as when the CIA supported the installation of Shah Reza Pahlavi's government in Iran, which created the conditions that ultimately made Iran one of the most anti-American nations in the region. As with military force, it is naive to think that external subversion is a reliable means of affecting the course of a nation's politics in a desired direction. Political reality is usually too complex to be shaped by the projects of foreign bureaucrats and covert operatives. And again, each time the United States engages in covert activity, it lends legitimacy to the practice of subversion by others, and we must ask whether U.S. interests would be best served if this were to become a universal instrument of foreign policy.

The broad conclusion may be that the world is not as simple or as malleable as political decision makers often believe. Many instruments of overt or covert coercion, even when applied by the most powerful nation in the world, are of limited use. The dilemma of effective choice bedevils the selection of foreign policy instruments, and even the selection of optimal goals. It may be hard to accept that the world cannot always be molded to suit our desires, but often more harm than good is done to the national interest by using ill-suited foreign policy instruments. This is an argument not for isolationism, but for good judgment and circumspection in making foreign policy.

National and International Prosperity

Prosperity is a goal of all societies, and governments understand that their continued incumbency may depend on their ability to deliver a satisfying level of material welfare to their publics. Since nations have become so economically interdependent, the fortunes of one affect the welfare of others, and international economic relations thus become permeated with political content. This interdependence and its political consequences have been considered in the context of U.S. relations with other industrialized democracies and in the context of its relations with the developing nations of the Third World.

Trade in the Developed World

International friendship rests on three conditions: an absence of fundamental incompatibilities of interest, a degree of positive interdependence for the achievement of national goals, and positive perceptions of each other, so that ambiguous actions will tend to be interpreted in a positive rather than a negative light. For the most part, these conditions have been obtained in the Western industrialized world, but certain strains have emerged, some of them political and some economic. The nations of the North Atlantic alliance have had different interpretations of Soviet behavior and different ideas about the appropriate responses, and their relations have also been marked by a certain amount of contention on issues of military burden-sharing. There have been economic problems as well, largely attributable to the slipping lead of the United States in the international economy and the domestic political pressures for protectionism that this has generated.

While it can be demonstrated that, in the long run, free trade benefits the international community as a whole, there are pressures that militate against unfettered economic relations, and these pressures are often imbedded in national politics. Politics thus intrudes into the economic realm, ensuring that optimal economic arrangements will often not be achieved. Within political democracies, groups that do not do well under conditions of open international competition seek to have the economy insulated from more efficient foreign producers, and political authorities are rarely willing to accept the electoral costs of ignoring these demands. In totalitarian systems, electoral pressures are not a problem; however, economic life is typically subordinated to state interests, and vulnerability to external economic conditions may be shunned for that reason—which may mean tightly controlled trading practices, though it may also mean that short-term economic losses are accepted in the expectation of long-term benefits.

In the United States and other industrial democracies, the accountability of governments for economic welfare and prosperity, and the short-term political horizons associated with electoral cycles, have provided an impetus toward neomercantilism. A weakening of the sense of common political purpose within the Western alliance is one of the potential consequences. To some degree, this may be inevitable, but it need not translate into a major threat to Western cooperation. The challenge is to maintain the problem within manageable boundaries. Partly, this requires special efforts at strengthening cooperation in noneconomic areas, but even more, it calls for measures to mitigate the economic problems. The loss of U.S. international economic dominance has been due largely to insufficient investment, especially in areas of new technology, and to excessive emphasis on quick profits, such as those that can be acquired from purchasing the assets of existing corporations (as witnessed in the "mergermania" of the 1980s). A solution to low productivity growth may be the adoption of an explicit industrial policy, involving active cooperation between business and government designed to steer the U.S. economy toward those areas in which it is likely to enjoy the greatest advantage in productivity compared to other nations. However, the conservative political mood of the 1980s is not conducive to so explicit a governmental participation in economic life.

Another challenge is to reduce the huge federal budget deficits, which have been financed by heavy government borrowing. This contributes to high interest rates, which in turn raise the cost of investment. Because of the high price of borrowing money, new investments are discouraged, hurting the nation's competitive position and the balance of trade. The solution must ultimately lie in the reduction of the deficits, either by increased taxes or by decreased public expenditures. Neither of these is politically popular, but they may be what statesmanship requires.

North-South Relations

Contrary to the usual perceptions, the developing world is not unilaterally dependent on the industrialized world. Although poor countries often depend on wealthy countries for economic assistance and investment, the economic well-being of the rich nations would be seriously impaired if they were deprived of the export markets which the developing nations provide; and several vital raw materials, some of which have strategic as well as economic significance, are obtainable only from Third World sources. Thus, rich and poor nations are linked by a symbiotic relationship, not one of supplicant and benefactor.

The economic policies of the United States vis-à-vis the developing world, including its programs of foreign assistance, have not been a product simply of beneficence. It may be assumed that most U.S. policy makers, like the public generally, wish the Third World well, but improvement in the standard of living of poor nations has not been the primary goal of policies on aid, trade, or investment. Foreign assistance has principally been an instrument of diplomatic and security leverage, rather than a subsidy for economic development. Trade and investment policies have served domestic rather than foreign economic interests. Perhaps the only exception has been assistance explicitly designed to enable a country to deal with a natural disaster, such as an earthquake or a drought.

Whatever the developed and developing nations may do, it is unlikely that many Third World nations will ever attain the standard of living now enjoyed by the United States or the nations of Western Europe, if for no other reason than because the earth's resource base could not sustain global levels of production comparable to those now found in the world's most affluent countries. Nevertheless, the developed world, and especially the United States, can do more to end or at least reduce poverty in the Third World than it has thus far done; and, by so doing, it can probably advance its foreign policy objectives more than by the short-term maneuvers and direct quid pro quos that have, for the most part, governed its economic dealings with the developing world.

The assumption of liberals that political stability will follow in the wake of rising standards of living may yet be borne out. A world less burdened by social and political turmoil would probably also be one in which pro-Soviet regimes would find it harder to obtain a foothold, and the U.S. national interest would benefit accordingly. Moreover, were the United States to replace its short-term pursuit of political advantage within the developing world by a policy of promoting Third World prosperity without strings attached, a more authentic and long-term identification with Western values could ensue. If the quid pro quo is the principal basis of U.S. policy in the Third World, support for U.S. values and interests will be no more stable than satisfaction with the short-term inducements. Hence, the long-term interests of the Third World and of the United States may actually be more convergent than U.S. foreign policy has so far assumed—and the dilemma of effective choice, in this regard at least, may be relatively easy to resolve.

The Issue of Human Rights

One stated objective of U.S. foreign policy has been to encourage respect abroad for the values that underlie its own political system—to make the world a more democratic place. The purpose of acquiring vast military power is often declared to be not merely the protection of narrow geopolitical or economic interests but the promotion of a set of political principles. Armed intervention is usually rationalized by the need to further democracy in the country to which the troops are dispatched. Economic assistance is justified in terms of its beneficial sociopolitical effects for the recipient society. The East-West struggle is cast in the apocalyptic mold of the defense of democratic virtue against totalitarian evil. Such lofty assertions lead us into the dilemma of political principle and raise two questions: To what extent does U.S. foreign policy truly embody the pursuit of democratic ideals in the world? To what extent is the promotion abroad of domestic political values an appropriate goal of U.S. foreign policy?

Policy Shifts

Until the mid-1970s, it was very hard to discern an authentic commitment to human rights as a foreign policy goal of the United States independent of geopolitical considerations. The strident anticommunism of the 1940s and 1950s was expressed in terms of the principles of freedom and democracy, but actually it could not easily be disentangled from the narrower politics of Cold War rivalry. Because the concern for human rights rarely went beyond denouncing their violations in the Soviet bloc—ignoring, for example, South Africa and several repressive Latin American regimes—it is hard to believe that liberty, rather than the competition with the Soviet Union, was the real issue. As one observer pointed out: "American anticommunism progressively became primarily not a moral crusade but a power struggle. And this power struggle came to outweigh competing values." [2]

The subordination of human rights to other diplomatic imperatives probably reached its apogee during the era of the Nixon-Kissinger foreign policy, when even the rhetoric of political principle was discarded and replaced by that of geopolitical interests and the search for a stable nuclear balance. Yet this posture had a certain objectivity to it, for it applied equally to dealings with friends and rivals. The military dictatorship in Greece (a NATO member) produced no frowns in the administration, nor did the brutality of dictatorships in countries such as Chile, Indonesia, Brazil, or Iran. By the same token, there was very little attempt to preach to the Soviet Union about human rights or to use the issue for Cold War propaganda purposes.

The first steps toward making human rights an independent policy objective came from the legislative branch. In 1974, Congress demanded that assistance be withheld from countries guilty of gross human rights violations, and this principle was reiterated in subsequent legislation. It is likely that congressional activism reflected a growing public unease with the systematic trampling on basic rights by nations with which the United States was closely associated. The gap between rhetoric and practice had become too great to ignore, and the national conscience was troubled.

With President Jimmy Carter's election, these qualms reached the executive branch as well. During the Carter administration, human rights occupied a more prominent place in U.S. foreign policy than they had before or have since. "Because we are free," the president said, "we can never be indifferent to the fate of freedom elsewhere." Unlike his predecessors, he rejected the temptation to equate anticommunist regimes with democratic regimes, and he declared:

> For too many years, we have been willing to adopt the flawed and erroneous principles of our adversaries, sometimes abandoning our own values for theirs. We have fought fire with fire, never thinking that fire is better quenched with water.... But through failure, we have now found our way back to our own principles and values.[3]

Carter directed his criticisms of human rights abuses at both Soviet-bloc nations and the undemocratic friends of the United States.

Critics, however, have cast doubt on the value of Carter's activism on behalf of human rights. It was naive, some said, to expect that the political practices of Soviet-style regimes would be affected by what a U.S. president chose to say about them; there were political realities too deeply entrenched to be affected by external verbal criticism. It was even feared that the Soviet Union might tighten internal repression in order to demonstrate its disregard for Washington's judgments. Some questioned the ability of the United States to change the practices even of those nations over which it did have leverage. According to a report prepared by the Congressional Research Service,

> the record on direct and explicit use of foreign assistance as leverage to bring about specific improvements in human rights conditions is hardly encouraging. In only five or six instances did we find evidence that actual or explicitly threatened reductions in aid played a significant role in bringing about changes in human rights conditions. Direct pressures seem often to provoke counterproductive reactions.[4]

Furthermore, the consequences of human rights activism for other foreign policy goals have been lamented as well—a case where the dilemmas of principle and of effective choice have overlapped. Advocates of East-West cooperation charged that the president's criticism of the Soviet human rights record perpetuated tension between the superpowers. Conservatives were critical of the policy's impact on the right-wing allies of the United States. Carter's decision to distance the United States from both the repressive regime of the Shah of Iran and the Somoza dictatorship in Nicaragua were said to have undermined both regimes and led to their replacement by a government of Islamic fundamentalists in the first case and of the Marxist Sandinistas in the second; neither of these was a model of democratic virtue, and, unlike their predecessors, both were virulently anti-American. Thus, according to conservative critics, democracy did not benefit from human rights activism, and foreign policy interests suffered considerably.

The climate changed significantly when the Reagan administration stepped into office. It agreed with those who did not feel that sanctions should be invoked against nations that supported U.S. foreign policy positions or at least pursued actively anticommunist policies. Human rights, in its view, should be used primarily as an anti-Soviet weapon. The Soviet Union was to be condemned for its lack of political liberties (among other things), while friends and allies, no matter how repressive, were to be spared any lectures on their political practices. In this respect, the Reagan administration reverted to the practice of using human rights mainly as a means of pursuing the Cold War.

What Role for Human Rights?

To what extent should the promotion of human rights be a goal of U.S. foreign policy? It has been argued that there is no justification for injecting values of this sort into foreign policy. According to George Kennan, one of the most thoughtful theorists of international relations, impulses that are appropriate to individuals are not necessarily appropriate to governments. A government's main duties, he says, are "military security, the integrity of its political life and the well-being of its people."[5] The promotion within other nations of the values a government is committed to domestically is not part of these responsibilities. Kennan recognizes that the United States has its own conception of political principles, but when other nations do not conform to these principles, he contends, it is not a matter of foreign policy concern unless it adversely affects U.S. *interests* (as opposed to its *values*). When the United States does protest against a nation's domestic political behavior, it should squarely recognize that its protest is motivated by national interest and not pretend to high-minded moralism. On the other hand, if the United States wishes to advance its conception of political ethics, it should do so by dint of its own behavior and example, not by impelling others to conform to its political tastes.

This argument is in many ways cogent, but it is not unassailable, and in any case the advice may not be practicable. The boundary between national interests and the promotion of political principles abroad is actually rather indistinct. Moreover, it may not always be possible to dissociate U.S. foreign policy from some sort of ethical framework if it is to receive adequate domestic support. For most Americans, a foreign policy is acceptable only if at least one of three conditions is met: (1) The policy must confer a direct personal benefit, (2) it has a clear and significant implication for the nation's security, and (3) it has an important moral dimension. But it is not often that identifiable personal interests are involved in foreign policy, and only a few issues have immediate and serious security implications. Accordingly, a nationally accepted moral value must be inolved if the policy is to receive support. In addition, many people in the United States want to believe that their country's power is part of some grand and elevated plan. As one of the nation's foremost historians has observed, "An Anglo-Saxon ancestry and a Calvinistic heritage have endowed Americans with a mighty need for seeing the exercise of power as morally virtuous." [6] Thus, there is an inclination to marry morality to power, and this often translates into the promotion abroad of lofty political principles.

Ethical considerations will probably never be entirely absent from either the rhetoric or the reality of U.S. foreign policy. By what criteria, then, should their application be guided? Two criteria seem especially important. One is the costs, including the diplomatic and security costs, of pursuing the policy in particular instances. The United States will usually alienate a regime whose human rights abuses it denounces, and this might or might not matter very much to U.S. national interests. The other is the probability of success. The United States does not have the same amount of leverage over all countries, and not all regimes are equally susceptible to outside pressure.

The problem, however, is that the application of these criteria is usually affected by ideological predilections. Typically, conservatives prefer that right-wing regimes be spared any criticism of their human rights abuses. According to the Reagan administration, for example, the nation's overriding security objective should be to weaken the Soviet Union, and human rights policies should not be allowed to interfere with this pursuit. Accordingly, a regime that is anticommunist should not be injured by criticism of its internal policies, and concern with political liberties should not be allowed to jeopardize the geopolitical advantage provided by a stable friend or ally. Sometimes this stance has been softened by making a distinction between repressive right-wing regimes, which are merely "authoritarian," and repressive leftist regimes, which are "totalitarian," the claim being that the abuses of the former are more tolerable than those of the latter. But this distinction is probably irrelevant from the point of view of the victims, and the fact remains that, in this perspective, human rights are subordinated to Cold War objectives.

From the point of view of many liberals, the primary security objective is to avoid nuclear war, and no other goal should be allowed to divert the country from this imperative. If human rights advocacy exacerbates Soviet-U.S. tensions, it is probably not worth pursuing. It is vital to establish stable and nonthreatening relations between the two superpowers, and denunciations of Soviet political practices are bound to make that more difficult.

It thus seems that the perceived costs of pursuing a human-rights policy in specific cases have depended essentially on attitudes toward the Soviet Union. But it would make sense to let this policy be guided at least as much by a conception of feasibility. If it would incur security costs of one kind or another, it should also be judged in the light of the chance that it will have some effect on the abusive political practices in question. While there is no guarantee that the United States can influence any nation's internal political practices, the likelihood that it can make a difference is obviously greater in nations over which it has some leverage. These are most often countries with which it has cordial security and economic relations, rather than those of the Soviet bloc.

Foreign policy is, as we have seen, a matter of solving problems in the absence of clear-cut solutions. In the United States, a leading source of frustration is the expectation that the most powerful nation on earth should be able to mold the world to its interests and tastes. But the international system is not that pliable, and the effects of foreign policy are too unpredictable. The reaction ought not be passivity but patience, an effort to think through the long-term implications of a contemplated policy rather than a reliance on facile recipes born of ideology, political expedience, or a superficial reading of history. Since resources are always limited, foreign policy should be directed primarily toward those crucial issues that it can indeed affect. Reducing the danger of nuclear war and controlling the expansion of strategic arsenals are among those issues.

U.S. foreign policy should also be guided by an appreciation of the economic interdependence of the world, of the need to cooperate with both the industrialized world and the developing nations, and of the benefits of keeping political and economic concerns as separate as possible. Finally, a nation as powerful as the United States must view its foreign policy not only in terms of what it does for its own people, but also in terms of its impact on the rest of the world's people as well. In many instances, both may be better served by doing less rather than more.

Notes

1. Norman Cousins, *The Pathology of Power* (New York: W. W. Norton, 1987), 184.
2. David P. Forsythe, *Human Rights and World Politics* (Lincoln: University of Nebraska Press, 1983), 89.
3. Jimmy Carter, "Humane Purposes in Foreign Policy," in *Human Rights and U.S. Foreign Policy,* ed. Barry M. Rubin and Elizabeth P. Spiro (Boulder, Colo.: Westview, 1979), 226-227.
4. Quoted in James R. Walczak, "New Directions in U.S. Food Aid: Human Rights and Economic Development," in *Global Human Rights: Public Policies, Comparative Measures, and NGO Strategies,* ed. Ved P. Nanda, James R. Scarritt, and George W. Sheperd, Jr. (Boulder, Colo.: Westview, 1981), 38.
5. George F. Kennan, "Morality and Foreign Policy," *Foreign Affairs* 86 (1985): 206.
6. Arthur M. Schlesinger, Jr., *The Cycles of American History* (Boston: Houghton Mifflin, 1986), 69.

Index

Abel, Elie, 129
ABM systems, 312, 313, 317, 318, 322
ABM Treaty, 38, 298, 303, 312, 313
"Accident Measures" Agreement, 329
Acheson, Dean, 85, 103, 310
Adelman, Kenneth L., 26
Aegean Sea, 275, 280
Afghanistan, 48
    Soviet invasion of, 40, 43, 44, 59, 65,
    74, 98, 127, 139, 180, 188, 196, 202,
    216, 299, 314
AFL/CIO, 132, 140, 141
Agricultural Trade Development Assis-
    tance Act, 102
Albania, 33, 156
Alcoa, 363
Alexander II, 28, 180
Alexander III, 29
Algeria, 360
Allen, Richard, 124
Allende, Salvador, 16, 68, 96, 136, 137,
    149
Alliance for Progress, 48, 358
Allison, Graham T., 52, 125
Almond, Gabriel, 52, 150
American Civil Liberties Union, 133
American Committee on East-West Ac-
    cord, 146
American Farm Bureau Federation, 139
American-Hellenic Institute, 143

American Institute for Imported Steel,
    149
American-Israel Public Affairs Commit-
    tee, 133, 142, 143, 149
American Jewish Committee, 142
American Petroleum Institute, 132, 135
American Security Council, 146
American Tobacco Institute, 132, 147
American Zionist Council, 142
Americans for Constitutional Action,
    145
Americans for Democratic Action, 145
Amin, Samir, 370
Anaconda Corporation, 136, 137, 363
Angola, 16, 39, 49, 93, 188, 200, 202, 277
Antarctic Treaty, 328
Antisubmarine warfare, 279, 280, 316
    and submarine sanctuaries, 279, 280
ANZUS Treaty, 223
Arbenz, Jacobo G., 19, 48, 116
Argentina, 363
Arms control, 310, 333, 380. See also
    specific agreements
    bureaucratic pressures and, 325, 326,
    328
    economic obstacles to, 326, 327, 328
    political climate and, 323-325, 328
    testing limitations and, 327, 328
    verification, 311, 314, 316
Arms Control Association, 146

Arms Export Control Act, 93, 101, 102, 121, 377
Arms race, causes
   action-reaction, 317, 318, 323, 325, 382
   bureaucratic pressures, 319, 320, 323, 325, 382
   domestic politics, 318, 319, 323, 352, 382
   economic interests, 321-323, 325, 382
   technological drives, 322, 323, 325, 382, 383
Aronson, Elliot, 175
Art, Robert J., 12, 13, 25, 129
Aspaturian, Vernon V., 203
Aspin, Les, 306
Austin, Anthony, 77, 103
Austin, Hudson, 232
Australia, 167, 205, 223, 271
Austria, 28
Austria-Hungary, 271
Axelrod, Robert, 172, 174, 175

Baker, Howard, 39, 94
Baker, James, 345
Balaguer, Joaquin, 231
Baldwin, David A., 370
Balkans, 155, 279
Ball, George, 242, 252, 278
Bamford, James, 129
Bangladesh, 353, 354
Baran, Paul, 160, 174
Barber, James D., 128
Barents Sea, 280
Barnet, Richard J., 150, 225
Barton, John H., 330
Baruch, Bernard, 310
Baruch Plan, 311
Basic Principles Agreement, 48, 200
Batista, Fulgencio, 235
Bayh, Birch, 143
Beer, Francis A., 175
Belgium, 42, 44, 271
Beres, Louis R., 281
Bergsten, Fred C., 361, 370
Berkowitz, Leonard, 174
Berlin crisis, 33, 35
Betts, Richard, 252
Bhagwati, Jagdish, 371
Bikini atol, 311
Biological Weapons Convention, 329
Bishop, Maurice, 232
Blainey, Geoffrey, 175

Blair, Bruce G., 330
Blake, David H., 350
Blechman, Barry M., 251, 252
Bloomfield, Lincoln, 106, 126
Bluestone, Barry, 350, 351
B'nai B'rith, 142
Bohlen, Charles E., 112, 129
Boland Amendment, 94, 101, 103, 121
Boland, Edward P., 94
Bolshevik Revolution. *See* Russian Revolution of 1917
Bosch, Juan, 48, 231
Bosporus Straits, 250
Boulding, Kenneth E., 174
Bourne, Kenneth, 175
Bracken, Paul, 281
Brandt Commission, 371
Brandt, Willy, 212, 225
Brazil, 67, 95, 96, 138, 363, 390
Bretton Woods agreement, 337, 338, 341
Brezhnev, Leonid, 49, 98, 314
Bricker, John, 94
Brodie, Bernard, 25
Brody, Richard A., 77
Broe, William, 137
"Broken Arrows," 263
Brown, Harold, 299
Brown, Michael B., 174
Brzezinski, Zbigniew, 120, 124
Bulgaria, 9, 33, 155, 166, 279
Bundy, McGeorge, 120
Bureaucracy and foreign policy, 106, 122, 123, 128, 378, 379. *See also* individual departments and agencies
Burke-Hartke bill. *See* Foreign Trade and Investment Act of 1972
Burma, 87
Burns, Arthur, 321
Burt, Richard, 281
Burton, John W., 25
Bush, George, 24
Business Roundtable, 135

Calleo, David, 350
Cambodia, 72, 75, 87, 92, 251
   U.S. invasion of, 245
Camp David accord, 14, 15, 274
Campbell, Angus, 77
Canada, 62, 66, 67, 167, 205, 209, 363
Cantril, Hedley, 76

Carter, Jimmy, 40, 64, 70, 93, 96, 106, 116, 117, 120, 124, 127, 139, 146, 236, 280, 299, 314, 394
Case Act, 95, 102, 377
Castro, Fidel, 16, 48, 64, 68, 235
Caterpillar Tractor Company, 214
Catherine the Great, 28, 180
Center for Defense Information, 146
Central Europe, 42, 43, 206, 355
  as possible war arena, 271-273, 276
  Soviet interests and, 271
  U.S. interests and, 271
Central Intelligence Agency (CIA), 18, 22, 89, 94, 100, 115, 116, 124, 147, 319, 378, 386
  director of central intelligence, 117
  involvement in Chile, 136, 137, 386
Challenger space shuttle, 263
Chambers, Whittaker, 111
Chamoun, Camille, 228, 229
Chernobyl, 263
Chiang Kai-shek, 187
Chile, 68, 96, 136, 137, 157, 185, 369, 386, 390
China lobby, 143
China, People's Republic of, 13, 14, 38, 40, 48, 67, 72, 81, 87, 121, 167, 185, 213, 221, 250, 289, 324
  and Korean War, 85, 86
Church, Frank, 107
Churchill, Winston, 31, 289
Circular error probable, 288
Civil War, U.S., 28
Clark Amendment, 102
Cnudde, Charles C., 26
Cognitive consistency, 163, 164, 209, 380
Cohen, Benjamin J., 53, 174
Cold War, 5, 28, 31, 32, 35, 41, 47, 49, 111, 117, 193, 212, 213, 216, 271, 284, 289, 310, 311, 336, 342, 355, 356, 359, 369, 383, 389
Collective goods, 218
Colombia, 353, 354
COMECON, 33, 212, 353
Comintern, 186
Commerce, Department of, 89, 108
Committee on the Present Danger, 133, 145, 146
Common Cause, 146, 147
Common Market, 45, 138, 169, 208, 212, 220, 340, 345

Common Agricultural Policy, 221, 343
Congo, 251
Congress, 79, 90, 101, 105, 106, 108, 127, 128, 376. *See also* Arms Export Control Act, Congressional Budget Office, Executive agreements, Foreign Assistance Act of 1975, Office of Technology Assessment, War Powers Act
  appointments, 82, 83, 88
  arms race and, 326
  arms sales and, 93
  budgetary control, 81, 82, 83
  executive branch and, 82, 84-90
  foreign trade and, 81
  House Un-American Activities Committee, 111
  treaties and, 80, 81, 88
Congressional Budget Office, 99
Constitution and foreign policy, 79, 80, 107
Containment policy, 233, 234, 238, 248. *See also* Cold War
  George Kennan and, 234
  Truman Doctrine, 234
Converse, Philip E., 77
Cooper, Richard N., 25, 350
Corwin, Edwin, 103
Cousins, Norman, 380, 394
Cox, Arthur M., 150, 200, 204, 282
Crabb, Cecil V., Jr., 103
Craig, Gordon, 174
Cruise missiles. *See* Nuclear weapons
Cuba, 12, 48, 64, 68, 116, 144, 184, 188, 195, 202, 232, 235, 250, 385
  U.S. economic sanctions and, 16, 17, 385
Cuban missile crisis, 75, 122, 277, 278, 311
Culbertson, John M., 225
Cusack, Thomas, 203, 330
Cyprus, 23, 143, 155
Czechoslovakia, 32, 33, 180
  Soviet invasion of, 13, 35, 196, 202, 212, 272, 279, 311, 355

Dahl, Robert A., 26, 103, 148, 150
Davis, Otto A., 330
Defense, Department of, 89, 112, 115, 124, 125, 192, 320. *See also* Joint Chiefs of Staff
  Defense Intelligence Agency, 117
  Department of the Air Force, 112

Department of the Army, 112
Department of the Navy, 112, 122
Marine Corps, 112
Office of International Security Affairs, 83, 114, 125
secretary of defense, 112
Special Forces, 235
Strategic Air Command, 124
De Gaulle, Charles, 212, 343
De Grasse, Robert W., Jr., 25, 203
Delors, Jacques, 222
Democracy, 20, 25, 375, 378. *See also*
Dilemmas of foreign policy
civil liberties and, 21, 22, 375, 378
electoral accountability, 21, 375
electoral politics and, 127
as foreign policy goal, 9, 10, 57, 98
interest groups and, 132, 147, 148
making of U.S. foreign policy and, 20
Dempster, M. A. H., 330
Denmark, 187
Dependency theory, 50, 51, 361-365
Destler, I. M., 77, 104, 350
Détente, 36-39, 40, 48, 142, 212, 216,
237, 299, 341, 359
Deutsch, Karl, 6, 25
Dewey, Thomas E., 139
Diem, Ngo Dinh, 91, 242
Dien Bien Phu, 241
Dilemmas of foreign policy, 23-25, 375
aggregation, 23, 79, 98, 123, 200, 375,
379
effective choice, 23, 79, 128, 247, 375,
384, 389
political principle, 24, 375, 379, 389
Diplomacy. *See* Foreign policy instruments
Dollar standards, 338
Dominican Republic, 48, 250
U.S. intervention in, 84, 202, 228, 231,
233, 236-238, 248, 251, 384
Dull, James, 129
Dulles, John Foster, 121, 196, 197, 247,
292, 306
Dumas, Lloyd J., 281

East Germany, 33, 211, 212, 272, 279,
355
Eastern Europe, 42, 71, 143, 166, 177,
196, 235, 289
Eberstein, William, 150
Eccles, Mariner S., 77
Ecuador, 360

Egypt, 9, 14, 15, 39, 48, 49, 67, 142, 229,
250, 273
Einhorn, Martin B., 330
Eisenhower, Dwight D., 35, 36, 71, 86,
103, 120-122, 126, 202, 228, 229, 294,
311, 321
administration of, 284, 292
Electromagnetic pulse (EMP), 257, 266,
273. *See also* Nuclear weapons
El Salvador, 16, 58, 97, 232
Ellsberg, Daniel, 245, 252
"Emergency Action Conferences," 264,
265
Engels, Friedrich, 184
Enthoven, Alan C., 307
Environmental Modification Convention, 329
Estonia, 180
Ethiopia, 39, 49, 72, 155, 188, 200, 202
European Coal and Steel Community,
44, 169
Exchange rates, 337
Executive agreements, 83, 84, 94
Executive branch. *See* Presidency, individual departments and agencies
Exports, 8
Exxon, 360

"Fail deadly," 266
Farnsworth, Clyde H., 203
Farnsworth, Elizabeth, 150
Federal Bureau of Investigation (FBI),
116
Federal Election Campaign Act, 134
Festinger, Leon A., 175
Fifth Eskadra, 275
Ford, Gerald R., 116, 121, 127, 298
Foreign Aid. *See* Foreign policy instruments, U.S. foreign assistance
Foreign Assistance Act of 1974, 102
Foreign Assistance Act of 1975, 97, 102
Foreign Assistance Act of 1976, 102
Foreign policy instruments, 10, 14
bribery, 14, 15, 17, 354, 385
diplomacy, 11, 12, 14-17, 359, 385
informal penetration, 16, 385, 386
military force, 11, 17, 385
Foreign policy objectives, 22
ideological, 5, 9, 22, 390
national security, 5, 22
prosperity, 5, 6, 22, 386
Foreign Service Officers, 111
Foreign Trade and Investment Act of
1972, 141

Forsythe, David P., 394
Foster, Gregory D., 129
France, 8, 9, 12, 29, 41, 42, 44, 46, 67, 166, 180, 187, 211, 213, 214, 216, 271, 324, 335, 353, 354
Franck, Thomas M., 103
Franco-Prussian War, 158, 324
Frank, Andre G., 370
Frankel, Max, 252
Free, Lloyd A., 76
Freedman, Lawrence, 306, 307
French Revolution, 162, 215
Freund, Gerald, 52
Fried, Morton, 174
Fulbright, William J., 91, 99, 104

Gabon, 360
Gaddis, John L., 252
Galbraith, John K., 330
Galtung, Johan, 370, 371
Gandhi, Mohandas, 47
Garcia-Mata, Carlos, 175
Gardner, John, 146
Garthoff, Raymond L., 302, 307
Garwin, Richard, 267, 314
Gelb, Leslie, 77, 104, 129, 252
Gemayel, Amin, 100, 230, 251
General Agreements on Tariffs and Trade (GATT), 337, 339, 342
General Electric, 214
George, Alexander, 175, 204
George III, 28
Geneva Conference (1954), 242
Geneva Protocol, 328
Gerard, Harold, 175
Gerrity, Edward, 137
Ghana, 50
Gibraltar, 155
Gilbert, George, 250
Gilbert, John H., 175
Gilpin, Robert, 350
Glorious Revolution, 215
Godoy, Hector G., 231
Golan Heights, 274
Gold, 334, 338
Golder, Frank A., 52
Goldman, Eric F., 129
Goldsborough, James O., 225
Goldwater, Barry, 127
Gorbachev, Mikhail, 191, 198, 203
Gosovic, Branislav, 53
Governmental bargaining model of foreign policy, 125

Graduated Reciprocation in Tension Reduction, 171-173
Gray, Colin, 300, 307
Great Britain, 5, 32, 40-42, 46, 62, 67, 68, 155, 205, 213, 215-217, 231, 273
Great Depression, 335
Great Rebellion, 215
Greece, 23, 142, 143, 155, 250, 273, 275, 279, 390
Greenstein, Fred I., 129
Grenada, 9, 12, 22, 72, 73
   U.S. invasion of, 197, 216, 228, 232, 233, 237, 238, 248, 251, 383, 384
Gromyko, Andrei, 64, 197, 203
Guatemala, 28, 48, 116. *See also* Informal penetration
Guinea-Bissau, 188
Gulf Oil Company, 360
Gulf of Tonkin, 72, 75, 86-88, 90, 92, 102
   Resolution, 242

Haas, Ernst B., 175
Haig, Alexander, 118, 124, 180, 237
Haiti, 251
Halberstam, David, 77, 252
Halle, Louis, 77
Halperin, Morton H., 129
Handlin, Mary F., 174
Handlin, Oscar, 174
Harris, Marvin, 174
Harrison, Bennett, 350, 351
Heilbroner, Robert, 350
Henkin, Louis, 103
Herken, Gregg, 306, 307, 330
Hilger, Gustav, 52
Hiroshima, 256, 262
Hitler, Adolf, 19, 30, 31, 132, 155, 156, 161, 166, 168, 271, 335
Hobson, J. A., 160, 174
Ho Chi Minh, 86, 242
Holsti, Ole, 196, 197, 203, 282
Holt, Pat, 103
Honduras, 58, 68, 94, 232, 236
Hostility, causes of, 154, 178. *See also* Cognitive consistency
   conflicts of interest, 154-157, 173
   dissimilarities, 154, 161, 162
   domestic needs, 154, 157-159, 173
   negative perceptions, 154, 163-166
Hot Line Agreement, 37, 312, 329
Hough, Jerry F., 204
Howe, Russell W., 150

Hughes, Barry B., 77, 150
Hughes-Ryan Amendment, 102
Human rights, 95, 390-393. *See also*
Congress
conservatives and, 392
Henry Kissinger and, 97, 390
Jimmy Carter and, 390
liberals and, 393
Ronald Reagan and, 97, 391
U.S. public and, 392
Hume, David, 334
Humphrey, Hubert, 70, 245
Hungary, 33, 35, 201, 272, 353, 354
Soviet invasion of, 196
Huntington, Samuel, 174, 370
Hymer, Stephen, 370

ICBMs, 264, 276, 287, 288, 294, 314
accuracy of, 269, 287, 288
launch procedures, U.S., 264
MARVs, 299
Midgetman, 285
Minuteman I, 285
Minuteman II, 285
Minuteman III, 268
MIRVs, Soviet, 312, 314
MIRVs, U.S., 268, 285, 298, 299, 313,
314, 318, 322, 323
MX, 267, 285, 299
SS-18, 268, 285
SS-25, 285
Titan I, 285
Titan II, 285
Immigration, 140
Imperialism, 159, 160, 197
India, 47, 48, 67, 68
Indonesia, 47, 48, 185, 250, 360, 390
Industrial policy, 347-349, 387
Inflation, 340
Informal penetration, 16, 17. *See also*
Central Intelligence Agency
CIA and, 18, 19
KGB and, 18
propaganda, 18
Radio Free Europe and, 18
Radio Liberty and, 18
USIA and, 18
Interest groups. *See also* Lobbies, Lob-
bying
defense producers, 136
democracy and, 132
U.S. foreign policy and, 131

International Bank for Reconstruction
and Development. *See* World Bank
International Development Act, 356
International friendship, 166, 205
absence of dissimilarities, 167, 387
nonconflicting interests, 166, 387
positive interdependence, 167-169,
173, 387
self-reinforcing perceptions, 170, 171,
387
International hostility. *See* Hostility
International Monetary Fund (IMF),
337, 338
Iran, 9, 32, 40, 47, 59, 62, 65, 67, 75, 94,
106, 116, 118, 155, 188, 201, 360, 386,
391
U.S. economic sanctions against, 16
Iran-contra affair, 101, 123, 124, 378,
379
Iran-Iraq War, 155, 274
Iraq, 155, 188, 360
Israel, 14, 15, 49, 67, 94, 133, 142, 182,
213, 229, 267, 273, 274, 275, 360
Italy, 9, 18, 40, 41, 44, 67, 206, 213, 214,
231
ITT, 134
involvement in Chile, 136, 137, 149
Ivan the Terrible, 180

Jackson, Henry M., 39, 98, 142
Jackson-Vanik Amendment, 143, 202
Janis, Irving, 175
Japan, 40, 66, 67, 156, 167, 205, 209,
213, 214, 215, 219, 221, 223, 273, 280,
288, 289, 333, 342, 346, 353, 354
economic competitor to U.S., 44, 45,
138, 206, 207, 220, 339, 340, 343,
344, 349
Javits, Jacob, 142, 143
Jefferson, Thomas, 109, 128
Jervis, Robert, 129, 163, 164, 175, 307
Johnson, Lyndon B., 9, 25, 37, 70, 71, 72,
73, 75, 87, 91, 107, 108, 120, 123, 127,
215, 231, 236, 243, 245, 246, 248, 340,
378
administration of, 341, 358, 377
Joint Chiefs of Staff, 112, 114, 125
Jones, Thomas, 228
Jordan, Hamilton, 118

Kane, Gordon L., 330
Kaplan, Fred M., 282, 306, 307
Katz, Arthur M., 281

Kaufmann, William, 174, 293, 307
Kearns, Doris, 252
Keeble, Curtis, 203
Kendal, Donald, 146
Kendal, Wilmoore, 26
Kennan, George F., 60, 61, 65, 76, 146,
    190, 203, 234, 252, 391, 394
Kennecott, 136, 137, 149
Kennedy, John F., 36, 37, 75, 87, 112,
    116, 120, 122, 123, 126, 139, 202, 233,
    235, 242, 245-247, 278, 294, 311, 358
    administration of, 358
Kennedy, Joseph, 159
Kennedy, Robert F., 91, 235
Kennedy Round agreements, 339, 344
KGB, 18. *See also* Informal penetration
Kenya, 8
Khrushchev, Nikita S., 47, 202, 235, 319,
    380
Kimche, David, 53
Kindleberger, Charles P., 169, 349, 351
Kirkpatrick, Jeane J., 25, 65
Kissinger, Henry K., 37-39, 52, 97, 98,
    111, 121, 124, 125, 129, 143, 192, 197,
    212, 288
Klare, Michael, 252
Klock, Donna J., 282
Koenig, Louis W., 128
Kolko, Gabriel, 252
Korean War, 73, 85, 228, 235, 238, 239,
    292, 310, 377, 383, 384. *See also* North
    Korea, South Korea
Kristol, Irving, 223, 225
Kugler, Jacek, 330
Kuwait, 360
Kwitny, Jonathan, 26
Ky, Nguyen Kao, 91

Labor, Department of, 89
Laos, 251
Lacqueur, Walter, 104
LaFeber, Walter, 52, 76, 103
Lake, Anthony, 77, 104
Laser-beam weapons, 286
Latin American Nuclear-Free Zone
    Treaty, 329
Latvia, 180
Lebanon, 75, 100, 216, 230, 274, 275
    1958 U.S. intervention, 84, 201, 228,
        233, 237, 238, 248, 250
    1983 U.S. intervention, 228, 233, 248
Lefever, Ernest W., 97, 104
LeMay, Curtis, 291

Lenczowski, John, 204
Lenin, Vladimir I., 160, 174, 184, 185,
    187
Libya, 9, 68, 360
    U.S. economic sanctions, 16
Lifton, Robert J., 281
Lilienthal, David, 310
Lincoln, Abraham, 28
Lindberg, Leon, 175
Lindzey, Gardner, 175
Lippmann, Walter, 24, 108
Lipton, Nancy, 330
Lithuania, 180
Lobbies. *See also* Interest groups, Lob-
    bying, individual lobbies
    business, 135-139, 147, 379
    ethnic, 142-144, 149, 379
    farm, 139, 140
    foreign, 144, 145
    labor, 140-142, 147, 379
    public interest, 145, 146
Lobbying, 133
    direct, 133
    indirect, 133
    dollar, 134
Louis XIV, 106
Lowi, Theodore J., 150
Lumumba, Patrice, 18
Luxemburg, 42, 44

MacArthur, Douglas, 85, 86, 87, 238,
    239, 252
MacFarland, Andrew S., 150
McCarthy, Eugene, 91, 245
McCarthy, Joseph R., 71, 111, 186, 241
McCloskey, Paul N., Jr., 77
McConnell, Grant, 150
McNamara, Robert, 294, 295, 296, 298,
    307, 371
McNaughton, John, 237
Magdoff, Harry, 252
Malaysia, 369
Malenkov, Georgi, 319
Manchuria, 181
Mandelbaum, Michael, 129, 255, 281
Manhattan Project, 22, 288
Mansfield, Mike, 126, 217
Mao Tse Tung, 111, 187
Marchetti, Victor, 26
Marcos, Ferdinand, 24, 96, 185
Marshall, George, 98, 129
Marshall Plan, 42, 90, 201, 339, 359
Marx, John D., 26

Marx, Karl, 184
Mathias, Charles, Jr., 76
Mathieson, John A., 371
Mayagüez, 251
Meany, George, 141
Meese, Edwin, 101
Melman, Seymour, 129
Mexico, 67, 138, 228, 359
Meyer, Alfred G., 52
Middle East War of 1948, 250
Middle East War of 1973, 7, 121, 360
Militarism, 160, 161
Military force. *See also* strategic doctrine
  compellence and, 13, 237, 383
  defense and, 12, 13, 383
  deterrence and, 12, 13, 237, 383
"Military-economic cycle," 321
Military-industrial complex, 193, 194, 382
Miller, Warren E., 77
Millikan, Max F., 370
Mills, C. Wright, 148, 150
Mitchell, John, 134
Moon, Parker T., 52
Moore, David W., 76
"Moral Majority," 145
Moreton, Edwina, 203
Morgenthau, Hans J., 25, 203
Mossadegh, Mohammed, 18, 116
"Most favored nation" principle, 337
MPLA, 93
Muller, Ronald E., 150
Multi-Fibre Agreement, 221, 343
Multilateral peacekeeping force, 230, 231
Multinational corporations, 8, 9, 51, 140, 141, 208, 340. *See also* Third World
Murphey, Robert, 174

Nacht, Michael, 203
Nagasaki, 256
Napoleon, 180, 271
Napoleonic wars, 162, 206
Nasser, Gamal Abdel, 187, 229
Nathan, James A., 129, 252, 306
National Association of Manufacturers, 135, 136
National Association of Wheat Growers, 139
National Commitments Resolution, 92, 95, 102

National Conservative Political Action Committee, 134
National Council for United States-China Trade, 135
National Farmers Union, 139
National Grange, 139
National Military Command Center, 264, 265
National Organization for Women, 133
National Rifle Association, 133
National Right to Life Committee, 133
National Security Act, 100, 112, 115, 118
National Security Agency, 116, 117
National Security Council, 101, 114, 116, 118, 120, 121, 125, 378. *See also* State Department
National Security Memorandum, 68
National Turkey Federation, 139
NATO, 33, 34, 43, 90, 201, 206, 207, 217-219, 224, 297, 333, 346
  burden sharing issue, 217-219
  tactical nuclear weapons and, 207, 271, 272, 278
  theater-nuclear weapons and, 217
Navarro, Peter, 150
Netherlands, 42, 44, 46
Nehru, Jawaharlal, 47
Neofunctionalism, 168, 169
Neomercantilism. *See* Protectionism
Neubauer, Deane E., 26
Neustadt, Richard, 129
New International Economic Order (NIEO), 51, 52, 365
  developed nations and, 366-367
  export prices, 366, 367
  foreign aid and, 365
  provisions of, 365, 366
New National Party, 233
New Zealand, 59, 167, 223
Newhouse, John, 330
Nicaragua, 16, 43, 59, 65, 67, 68, 94, 96, 108, 185, 188, 216, 228, 385, 391
Nicholson, Harold G., 25
Nigeria, 67, 360
Nincic, Miroslav, 25, 26, 174, 203, 282, 330
Nitze, Paul, 145, 146
Nixon, Richard M., 39, 49, 70, 75, 91, 95, 98, 118, 120-122, 126, 127, 134, 139, 141, 142, 179, 203, 212, 236, 241, 245, 247, 321, 330, 341, 342
  administration of, 377, 378
Nkrumah, Kwame, 50, 53

Nunn, Sam, 218
NORAD, 264, 265
North, Oliver, 123
North Korea, 68, 85, 158, 241, 276, 277.
 See also Korean War
North Vietnam, 9, 12, 75, 86, 91, 92,
 121. *See also* Vietnam War
 U.S. bombing of, 242, 243, 245
Norway, 166
Nuclear Nonproliferation Treaty, 312,
 329
Nuclear war, 255-276, 380. *See also*
 Nuclear weapons, Strategic doctrine
 collapse of democracy and, 263
 compared to conventional war, 255
 as consequence of escalation of conventional conflict, 262, 381
 as consequence of preemptive first
 use, 262, 266-270, 381
 as consequence of system malfunction, 262, 263, 280, 381
 as consequence of unauthorized initiation, 262, 264-266, 381
 destruction of agriculture and, 260
 destruction of manufacturing capacity
 and, 259-260
 destruction of population and, 257,
 258
 hot line and, 277, 278
 limiting, 300-303, 381
 nuclear weapon-free zones and, 278-
 279, 281
 nuclear winter and, 260, 261
 possibility of in Central Europe, 271-
 273, 381
 possibility of in Middle East, 273-276,
 381
 psycho-social effects, 261
 submarine invulnerability and, 279-
 280
 superpower diplomacy and, 276, 277
Nuclear weapons, 6, 13, 282. *See also*
 ICBMs, Nuclear war, SLBMs, Strategic
 bombers, Strategic doctrine
 blast effects, 256, 257, 300
 command and control, 272
 cruise missiles, 285, 299, 315-317
 first Soviet use, 256
 first U.S. use, 256
 fission, 256, 284
 fusion, 256, 284

Occidental Petroleum, 360
O'Donnell, Kenneth, 252

Office of Technology Assessment, 99,
 307
Ogaden War, 155
Ohlin, Goran, 370
Oliver, James K., 129, 252, 306
Olson, Mancur, 225
OPEC, 360, 361, 367, 368
Organization of American States (OAS),
 231
Organization for Economic Cooperation
 and Development (OECD), 167, 208,
 336, 353
Organization for European Economic
 Cooperation (OEEC), 42
Organizational process model of foreign
 policy, 125
Organski, A.F.K., 330
Osgood, Charles, 171, 175
Outer Space Treaty, 328

Packwood, Bob, 222
Page, Benjamin I., 77
Pahlavi, Reza (Shah), 19, 116, 386
Palestine Liberation Organization
 (PLO), 229
Palme, Olof, 215
Palmerston, Henry T., 163
Panama Canal zone, 236
Panama Canal Treaty, 81, 134
Paris Commune, 158
Park, Tongsun, 145
Partial Test Ban Treaty, 37, 312, 328
Particle-beam weapons, 286
Pathet Lao, 251
Payne, Keith, 307
Peace Corps, 358
Peaceful Nuclear Explosions Treaty, 329
Pennock, Ronald J., 26
Pentagon. *See* Defense, Department of
Persian Gulf, 7, 40, 65, 100, 236, 249,
 251, 273, 360
Peru, 59, 166
Peter the Great, 180
Petras, James, 150
Philippines, 15, 24, 67, 96, 185
Pierre, Andrew J., 104
Pinochet, Augusto, 137, 185
Pipes, Richard, 179, 187, 189, 203
Podhoretz, Norman, 61, 76, 77
Poindexter, John, 121, 123
Poland, 8, 17, 31-33, 67, 139, 180, 212,
 213, 272, 355

Political action committees (PACs), 134, 135, 139. *See also* Lobbies
Porro, Jeffrey D., 307
Portugal, 46
Potsdam Agreement, 84
Presidency, 79, 105-108, 121, 123, 126, 128
  Executive Office of the President, 118
  treaty powers, 107
  war powers and, 80
  White House Office, 118
Presidential Directive 59, 299, 302
Prevention of Nuclear War Agreement, 329
Prewitt, Kenneth, 150
Pringle, H. F., 52
Progressivism, 148
Protectionism, 24, 149, 219-222, 336, 341, 343, 346, 349, 387
  "infant industries" and, 356, 357
  nontariff barriers and, 344
  quotas and, 336, 339
  tariffs and, 336, 339
Protective action link, 272
Prussia, 28
Public Law 480, 139

Qatar, 360
Quemoy, 250

Rail gun, 286, 304
Ranney, Austin, 26
Rappoport, Anatol, 174
Rational actor model of foreign policy, 125
Ravenal, Earl C., 225
Reagan, Ronald, 40, 63, 70, 71, 84, 89, 94, 97, 108, 116, 117, 120, 121, 124, 126, 127, 143, 202, 203, 221, 222, 230, 286, 302, 314, 379
  administration of, 23, 83, 101, 125, 138, 164, 213, 236, 299
Reform Bill, 215
Reich, Robert, 350
Reilly, John E., 67, 76
Ribicoff, Abraham, 142
Ricardo, David, 335, 342
Ridgway, Matthew, 241
Robinson, James A., 103
Rodberg, Leonard S., 330
Rogers, William, 124
Rohatyn, Felix, 348, 351
Romania, 33, 180, 188, 279

Roosevelt, Franklin D., 30, 71, 73, 112
Rosenau, James N., 59, 65, 76, 175
Rostow, Eugene, 145, 146
Rostow, Walt W., 242, 370
Royal-Dutch Shell, 300
Rusk, Dean, 120, 282
Russell, Richard, 246
Russett, Bruce M., 76, 307, 330
Russian Revolution of 1917, 29, 30, 186, 194, 197

Salisbury, Robert, 159
SALT I, 38, 311-314, 316
  ABM Treaty, 312-313, 329
  Interim Offensive Arms Agreement, 312-313, 329
SALT II, 39, 81, 133, 314, 315, 316, 329, 333
Samuelson, Paul A., 350
Sandino, Augusto, 228
SANE, 146
Santos, Theotonio dos, 371
Saudi Arabia, 67, 94, 143, 353, 354, 360
Scheider, Steven H., 281
Scheingold, Stuart, 175
Schlesinger, Arthur, Jr., 128, 129, 245, 252, 394
Schlesinger, James, 192, 297
Schmitter, Philippe, 175
Scigliano, Robert, 252
Scotland, 312
Scowcroft, Brent, 124
Sea of Okhotsk, 280
Seabed Arms Control Treaty, 329
Serbia, 271
Seton-Watson, Hugh, 53
Sewell, John P., 371
Shafer, Michael, 203
Shaw, Albert, 25
Shawcross, William, 77, 103, 252
Shearer, Derek, 330
Shipler, David K., 203
Short, Dewey, 241
Shultz, George, 64, 100, 121, 123, 124, 192
Sigal, Leon, 307
Simes, Dimitri K., 212, 225
Singapore, 49
Singer, David, 175, 282
SLBMs, 264, 276, 287, 288. *See also* Nuclear war, Nuclear weapons
  accuracy of, 269
  D-5, 299

ICBM compared to, 270
invulnerability of, 269-270, 288, 295
launch procedures, 264, 265
Polaris, 320
Smith, Adam, 168, 335, 342
Smith, Alexander, 85
Smith, Hedrick, 76, 252
Smith, Wayne, 307
Smoot-Hawley Act, 335
Somalia, 72, 155, 202
Somoza, Anastasio, 96, 185
South Africa, 11, 17, 23, 67, 138, 164, 183, 215
South Korea, 45, 47, 49, 67, 68, 85, 138, 145, 158, 207, 276, 277, 359. *See also* Korean War
South Vietnam, 13, 86, 88, 95, 127. *See also* Vietnam War
Soviet Union, 9, 12, 13, 27, 72, 81, 86, 96, 156, 166, 167, 171, 212, 234. *See also* Cold War, Détente, U.S.-Soviet relations
  economic performance, 38, 190, 191
  expansionism and, 179, 180
  human rights, 40, 390
  ideological tenets, 184, 185
  inferiority feeling toward West, 189, 190
  need for Western technology, 182
  perceptions of the United States, 197, 198
  Third World and, 47
  U.S. conservative views of, 177, 178
  U.S. liberal views of, 178
  U.S. public's perception of, 61-64, 67
Spain, 40, 46, 155, 312
Spanier, John, 252
Spanish-American War, 195
Sprague, Robert, 291
Sputnik, 294, 320
Stabex system, 366, 367
Stalin, Joseph, 30, 31, 43, 132, 187, 201, 235, 289, 357
"Star Wars," 202, 304, 309, 315-317
  arguments for, 305
  criticism of, 305, 306
  technical requirements, 304
  Western Europe and, 305
Starr, Harvey, 197, 203
State, Department of, 89, 109, 111, 112, 121, 122, 124, 137, 192
  Agency for International Development, 89, 109, 357, 358

Arms Control and Disarmament Agency, 89, 109, 124, 146, 309
  Bureau of Intelligence and Research, 117, 229
  Bureau of Politico-Military Affairs, 109, 114
  U.S. Information Agency, 89, 109
Stebbins, Richard P., 129
Steel, Ronald, 129
Steele, Jonathan, 203
Stevenson, Adlai, 71
Stockwell, John, 26
Stoessinger, John G., 52
Stokes, Donald E., 77
Stone, Alan, 150
Strange, Susan, 350
Strategic Air Command, 264, 265
Strategic bombers, 264, 276, 287, 288. *See also* Nuclear weapons
  B1-B, 285
  B-29, 292
  B-42, 293
  B-45, 293
  B-50, 292
  Bear, 293
  Bison, 293
  stealth, 285
Strategic Defense Initiative (SDI). *See* "Star Wars"
Strategic Doctrine, 13, 328. *See also* Nuclear war, Nuclear weapons, Presidential Directive 59, "Star Wars"
  counterforce, 291, 296, 298, 300-305
  countervalue, 291, 295, 296
  escalation dominance, 297, 298, 300
  first use, 291
  flexible response, 294, 295
  MAD, 295-300, 313
  massive retaliation, 291, 292, 294, 295, 297, 298
  nuclear war fighting and, 296, 298
  preemptive strike and, 294, 295, 300
  second strike and, 295, 296
  Soviet Union and, 301, 302
Sukarno, Achmed, 47
Sundquist, James L., 103
Symington, Stuart, 95
Sweden, 166, 180, 215
Sweezy, Paul, 160, 174
Syria, 39, 48, 67, 229, 230, 273-275

Taft, Robert, 111
Taiwan, 35, 49, 67, 142, 143, 207, 250, 359

Talbott, Strobe, 330
"Tallinn Line," 317, 318
Taubman, William, 326, 330
Taylor, Maxwell, 242
Teamsters, 140
Texas, 180, 227
Thailand, 87, 251, 353, 354, 359
Thatcher, Margaret, 214, 216
Thibault, George, 129
Thies, Wallace J., 252
Thieu, Nguyen Van, 95
Third World, 27, 45, 47, 249. *See also*
　Dependency theory, New International
　Economic Order, Stabex, U.S. foreign
　assistance, U.S. military interventions
　in Third World
　colonialism and, 46, 354, 362
　economic activism and, 360, 361
　export earnings of, 363, 364, 366
　foreign investment in, 362-364
　nonaligned movement and, 46
　terms of trade, 362, 364
　trade preferences and, 357
　U.S.-Soviet rivalry in, 48, 187, 188,
　　199, 234, 354, 356, 368, 369, 380
Thirty-Year War, 162, 206
Thucydides, 281
Thompson, Stanley L., 281
Three Mile Island, 263
Threshold Test Ban Treaty, 329
Thurow, Lester, 222, 225, 346, 350
Tillema, Herbert K., 251
Tocqueville, Alexis de, 24, 26, 58, 76,
　131, 150
Tokes, Rudolf, 330
Trade Reform Act of 1974, 143, 343
Treasury, Department of, 89, 108, 137
Treaty of Brussels, 42
Treaty of Versailles, 83, 89
Treaty of Westphalia, 206
Trieste, 249, 250
Trott, Sarah H., 150
Trujillo, Rafael, 231
Truman, Harry S, 32, 33, 71, 73, 103,
　122, 139, 234, 239, 247, 284, 289
Truman Doctrine, 201
Tsipis, Kosta, 281, 282, 306
Tufte, Edward, 330
Turkey, 23, 32, 47, 122, 142-144, 155,
　201, 234, 272, 273, 275, 279
Turkish Straits, 275
Turner, Stanfield, 129
Twain, Mark, 29

U-2 incident, 35, 36, 202, 311
Uganda, 185
Union of Concerned Scientists, 146
United Arab Emirates, 360
United Autoworkers, 133, 140
United Brands, 363
United Mine Workers, 140
United Nations, 85, 310
United Nations Association, 145
U.S. balance of payments, 340, 341
U.S. Central Command, 236
U.S. Chamber of Commerce, 133, 135
U.S. Development Assistance Loan
　Fund, 357
U.S. economic productivity, 221, 222,
　346, 347
U.S. foreign assistance, 258, 388, 389.
　See also Alliance for Progress, Marshall
　Plan, Peace Corps
　Cold War goals and, 358-361
　John F. Kennedy and, 357-358
　Lyndon B. Johnson and, 358
U.S.-Japan Trade Council, 144
U.S.-Mexican War, 227
U.S. military interventions in Third
　World, 84-88, 227, 236. *See also* indi-
　vidual countries
　credibility and, 246-248
　domestic politics and, 247, 248
　quagmire theory of, 245
　stalemate machine and, 245
　sunken costs and, 246, 248
U.S. Sixth Fleet, 275
U.S.-Soviet relations, 28, 29, 31, 33, 36,
　37, 39, 127, 379. *See also* Arms race,
　Arms control, Cold War, Détente,
　Third World
　bureaucratic pressure and, 190-193
　circumventing hostility, 324, 325
　controlling hostility, 324, 325
　domestic politics and, 189-190, 192,
　　199, 325
　economic influences and, 193, 194,
　　199
　objective conflicts of interest and,
　　179-181, 184, 199, 200, 379
U.S.-Soviet strategic balance, 286-288
Uruguay, 8
Ury, William, 282

Vance, Cyrus, 120, 124
Venezuela, 166, 250, 360

Verba, Sidney, 150
Vernon, Raymond, 350
Viet Cong, 86, 90, 242
Vietnam War, 72, 73, 80, 90, 91, 95, 99, 107, 108, 116, 128, 141, 146, 147, 198, 200, 202, 215, 220, 228, 236-238, 241, 246-248, 299, 340, 359, 377, 378, 383, 384
    termination of, 245
    Tet offensive, 243
Viguerie, Richard, 134
Vladivostok Accord, 39, 202
Vogel, Ezra, 350
von Bulow, Bernard, 271

Walczak, James R., 394
Wallensteen, Peter, 26
Walter, Robert S., 53, 350
Warnke, Paul, 146
War Powers Act, 92, 99, 100, 102, 377
Warsaw Pact, 34, 219, 279
Washington, George, 43, 84
Watson, Russell, 104
Weiler, Lawrence D., 330
Weinberger, Caspar, 192, 281
Weisband, Edward, 103
Weisberger, Bernard A., 103, 129
Weissberg, Robert, 76
West Germany, 30-32, 34, 41, 44, 66, 67, 166, 211, 213, 215, 217, 272, 279, 324, 346, 355
Western alliance. *See also* NATO
    absence of fundamental dissimilarities, 208-209
    attitudes toward Soviet Union, 210-213, 215, 216, 223
    differences in political practice within, 208-209
    economic interdependence in, 205, 206
    nonconflicting interests in, 205, 206
    security interdependence in, 206
    self-perpetuating perceptions in, 209-210

Western Europe, 41-43, 166, 169, 203, 206, 207, 213, 219, 223, 273, 338, 342. *See also* Common Market, NATO, Western alliance
    economic competition with United States, 44, 45, 138, 206, 220, 340, 349
Westmoreland, William, 88, 243
Wicker, Tom, 103
Wilcox, Clair, 350
Wildavsky, Aaron, 26, 129, 330
Wilson, Harold, 215
Wilson, Woodrow, 9, 30
"Window of vulnerability," 267, 268
Wit, Joel, 282
Wohlstetter, Albert, 296, 330
World Bank, 137, 338, 357
    International Finance Corporation, 357
    International Development Association, 357
World Federalists, 145
World War I, 40, 46, 90, 158, 206, 227, 228, 270, 310, 324, 336, 340
World War II, 31, 40, 41, 84, 90, 168, 170, 195, 206, 227, 228, 255, 296, 310, 324, 336, 340, 349, 355, 383
Wright, Quincy, 157, 158, 174

Yalta Conference, 32, 84, 201
Yalu River, 239
Yarmolinski, Adam, 129, 326
York, Herbert, 330
Yugoslavia, 33, 43, 72, 155, 167, 185, 188, 213, 250, 279, 353, 354

Zadny, Jerzy, 175
Zaire, 181, 184
Zajonc, Robert, 175
Zambia, 50, 184, 353, 354
Zartman, William E., 25
Zeckhauser, Richard, 225
Zimbabwe, 72, 183, 188, 369